The
Vice
President
The Trillionaire

CAROLINADEIVID

TOUCH
LADYBIRD
LUCKY
STUDIOS

A CAROLINADEIVID PRODUCTION 2018

DEDICATION

To wisdom, foresight, courage, accountability and the
endless search of riches.

DISCLAIMER

This is a work of fiction. Names, characters, businesses, places, events, and incidents are either the products of the author's imagination or used in a fictitious manner. Any resemblance to actual persons, living or dead, or actual events is purely coincidental.

ACKNOWLEDGMENTS

Many thanks and best wishes to the Carolinadeivid brand. Big thanks also to Touchladybirdlucky Studios.

The Vice President The Trillionaire

CHAPTER ONE

A reindeer struggled to free itself trapped in the icy-waters. Exhausted, cold, and petrified it glanced around for a while knees deep in the icy-waters. It spewed out steamy breath through its nostrils into the cold icy air. A bird circled above in the sky catching the attention of the troubled animal. For a moment or two, it seemed the reindeer had forgotten its troubles as it succumbed to the grip of the frozen icy water. For a minute the reindeer forgot all its troubles, and it stared at the bird. The icy-water caused such a sting that the reindeer struggled with all the energy it had freeing one of the trapped front legs. After hopping out one of its legs out of the icy-waters, the reindeer stopped and threw a quick glance at the surrounding bushes. Instantly a deafening outcry was heard coming from the surrounding bushes. A female reindeer stood there looking hopeless not knowing what to do. Something was awry. This cry would have committed the male reindeer running toward the female one in no time. This was a desperate cry. A call for help yet the male reindeer was nowhere to be seen. It was extremely cold in the forest in one of Russia's cities. The second cry sends the male reindeer fighting for its life. This was a grave affair. Many animals had perished in these icy-waters. The temperatures were below freezing point. Yes, it was winter in Russia, excessively cold and perhaps the worst time of many of the creatures. Scarce food, wintry conditions, and many dangers. The third cry from the female reindeer jump-started the male reindeer into action. The reindeer fought the icy-waters and hobbled out first tumbling down on its knees unable to move before letting out a raucous moan that startled the few birds in the surrounding trees. One of the birds flew over the icy river waters to the other side and past a house not far away. The entire land was buried in ice. In a short distance away, a red land-rover slowly drove on the icy-land heading toward the detached house. Inside the house, an enormous wolf-dog started barking and wagging its tail. A young blond girl rushed downstairs toward the door pushing the wolf-dog aside before opening the door. Violet who was upstairs shouted something to her daughter Kate. That fell on deaf ears as the girl proceeded on to open the door without hesitation. She looked outside before sprinting toward a red land rover that was still far away. Kate was about five or six years old. She braced the freezing weather and dashed toward the car with her blond hair streaming backward. Soon after the wolf-dog brushed against the little girl wriggling its tail in hysteria. The little girl stumbled to the ground as the wolf-dog sped past her. Kate immediately got up and continued running toward the approaching red land rover. The wolf-dog stopped for a while and gazed backward at Kate before sprinting toward the car.

"Be careful!" yelled Violet standing at the door of the house. The man in the car smiled as he drove the land rover slowly toward the house. Immediately the wolf-dog jumped onto the bonnet of the car and the man abruptly halted the car and smiled. Quickly he got out of the car and the wolf-dog jumped onto his legs wriggling its tail. The man knelt rubbing the wolf-dog's head and body.

"Daddy, daddy," cried the young blond girl running toward the man and the wolf-dog. The man got up and ran toward the girl with open arms.

"Daddy!" screamed the young girl.

"My angel I miss you very much," shouted the man picking up the young girl into the freezing air and swinging around holding the girl up. Emotionally the girl held tight to her dad. The dog wriggled its tail and rubbed itself against the man barking enthusiastically. The man kissed the girl on the forehead and on her very pronounced dimples. The woman stood on the veranda of the house waving in excitement. The wolf-dog soon sprinted toward the woman leaving behind the father and daughter as they approached the house. Later that evening the family gathered in the living room watching the television.

"So how has it been? What did the doctors say?" inquired the wife.

"Nothing much but since the accident, my leg has been giving me too much pain. Maybe I should go for X-rays." In one of the big cities in the United States, a woman stood at the window staring outside. She slowly sipped her wine looking outside. It was freezing. She glanced outside admiring the exquisite garden and swiftly a heavily armed security guard passed the window and instantaneously there was a loud knock. The woman very elegantly dressed in a female suit walked toward the table and placed the wine glass down before answering the door.

"Come in."

Quickly the heavy wooden door opened and a hand wearing white clean gloves held the middle of the door and pushed the door open.

"Sorry to disturb you but you have a visitor. He said it's important." Instantly a man appeared on the door wearing an expensive blue suit with a long white tie. The woman signaled the man in and shortly thereafter the huge door shut behind them. The two walked toward the big table. The man stopped and threw a quick glance around the office.

"Very impressive."

"Thank you," acknowledged the woman picking up the wine glass.

"What brings you here?" inquired the woman. The man touched his white tie before sitting down caressing it gently.

"I need you to let out this lady with immediate effect." The woman ignored the man's pleas.

"Release this lady today."

The woman sat down and suddenly leaned forward.

"My hands are tied after all she committed a crime."

"I don't care. You murdered her father." "Am I a drug dealer or a heroin pusher? Be careful what you say to me. I take that as an insult," retorted the woman bitterly. "Don't be a smart ass with me."

"I have clean hands. I wasn't involved in whatever happened to him."

"Why is it that everyone linked to you end up on drugs or dead?" Quizzed the man with a suspicious face.

"Just a coincidence. My hands are clean." "You are not taking me seriously."

"Are you threatening me? I could have had you executed anytime you know?"

"Me, your sitting duck? Think again."

The woman gave a sardonic laugh and stood up. She walked toward the window and glanced outside before menacingly staring at the man who was seated on his sofa. "You got nothing against me. You think I am stupid?"

"Ooh, you think you are a very clever mind you once bitten twice shy."

"What do you want? How much you want? You think you can blackmail me? You won't even have the chance to spend the money. I will just snap my fingers and you are dead meat for a fraction of that money."

"Please! I don't want your bloody money."

"So, what-the-fuck you want?" The man stood up and walked toward the window. He briefly stared outside before replying without looking at the woman.

"I want this lady freed and compensated for the loss of her father." She threw a quick glance at him and grinned before sitting down.

"I don't work that way. Will you excuse me I have no time for this?" Requested the woman whilst giving the man an evil eye. "I am not bluffing. I want this woman out or else you will regret it." The woman laughed sarcastically and slowly sipped her wine.

"You got nothing against me like I said." There was a moment of silence. The man briefly looked outside.

"I sent the file to the FBI, and it's just a phone call away and you are as good as buried." The woman grinned mockingly and stared at the man.

"I don't leave dirty behind."

"I know," replied the man calm and confident.

"So?"

"Let's put it this way. I am just ahead of my times if you know what I mean," replied the man boastfully before sitting back on his sofa. The woman scoffed and gave the man an evil eye.

"If you don't have anything else to say I am kind of busy." The man looked annoyed and felt agitated before he stood up. "Alright maybe talk to the FBI." The man dipped his hand in his trousers pocket and took out a phone and dialed a number and activated the speaker button. An automated voice came up.

"You have reached the Federal Bureau of Investigation please listen and choose the correct option." The man threw a quick glance and smiled cheekily. The woman's face sunk and quickly she looked outside through the window before turning around.

"OK, what do you have against me?"

"All our conversations and findings."

"Still that can't prove anything."

"Just enough to prove that you framed the poor girl and set her up after killing her father just to cover your back, you, cold-blooded killer."

"I take threats very seriously Mr."

"Not just an empty threat. I want this lady free you heard me." There was a moment of silence.

"I want your word, or I am going to send you to hell."

"What do you want from me? Money?" "Like I said I don't want your filthy money. Just this lady free or else you face the consequences." The woman scoffed. "You don't know me very well. Like I said I take threats very seriously." The man looked annoyed and unmoved.

"The feeling is mutual." The man paused before continuing.

"Or else you will be drinking this wine in hell." The woman instantly squirted out the wine she was about to swallow and mockingly laughed at the man. Instantly her face blushed with rage and anger that her face wrinkled up.

"You son of a bitch! Make up your mind. I told you from the beginning it's either you or her. You forgot already? Just a few months ago you begged me to spare you. You said I should spare you and kill this lady. What do you want? It's either you or this lady. You are telling me that you want to waste your life for this silly lady?"

"I am not a murderer. I am not like you. I am not a scumbag."

"You arrogant cold-blooded killer, just because you couldn't finish her off that doesn't make you an angel. Remember it's either obey or die."

"I will never be like you. A bloody monster. When are you going to stop?" "Please! You were zealous to kill her now you want to pretend that you care."

"FBI or the lady is free and safe," silence broke out before the woman replied.

"Give me time she committed a crime I can't just do as I please."

"But you can murder her father and frame her?"

"Leave this to me."

"Not good enough. I want your word that she will be out today." A cat was sleeping under a car in one of the suburbs. It was sunny. The cat dawdled staggering toward the shadow of the bird which shortly disappeared. The cat stood for a while and lazily looked around. A car suddenly appeared from nowhere and nearly crashed the cat as it crossed the road. The cat proceeded toward a huge playing ground and disappeared for a while. Not far away from the fields were huge buildings with football and basketball pitches. This looked like a school. The cat soon reappeared and crossed one of the pitches and headed toward one of the buildings. Soon it was outside the window seal of one of the buildings. It meowed and looked inside. One of the ladies in the classroom looked at the cat and poked her friend sitting next to her before pointing at the cat. The cat meowed and scratched the window as if it wanted to get in. The teacher stopped and first looked at the lady giggling and disturbing her friend before the cat caught his attention too. Soon after the cat disappeared, and the teacher continued with his lesson. After the cat incident, every one of the pupils listened to the teacher attentively. Minutes later, a folded paper plane landed on Nicodem's desk. Instantly he picked up the folded paper plane and looked at the teacher first, then at one of the ladies next to him and then quickly opened the folded small paper. He read it and looked at one of the beautiful ladies in his class. The lady was such a stunner. She had lovely long blonde hair, with a face of a goddess, everything was perfect in place, with much-pronounced dimples that every facial movement left these dimples well pronounced. Her smile was that infectious that just one look at her you would feel like smiling too. Everything about her was addictive and everything was just ecstasy. The young man looked at the lady. She whispered something to him. He did not get even a word that she said. He was overwhelmingly excited wondering how God was showing off when he created her. The looks, those shining blue eyes, the lovely blonde hair, and the sexy adorable smile with those cheeky dimples, I mean everything made her look like an angel. The young man stopped daydreaming and took notice only when the lady got up and pulled her blouse down at the same time lifting her blessed chest showing the biggest yet perfect assets a woman can possess. He opened his eyes and mouth simultaneously before the lady giggled. Immediately the young man's attention was drawn toward the lady's face as her white shining teeth caught his attention. Puzzled and mesmerized the young man looked at the lady as she pointed toward the door with her glittering watery blue eyes. The young man looked lost for a while. He threw a quick glance at the teacher and the whole class. The lady smiled again flashing her teeth and making her dimples very much pronounced. She threw a quick glance at the young man simultaneously pulling down her blouse before she started strolling toward the door before disappearing. The young man gazed at everyone and then the teacher and instantly stood up and stealthily followed the lady out of the classroom. Seconds later, two giggling voices were heard outside the class and soon after that, the voices faded away.

"Where are you going?"

"To the library, I need some books."

"In the middle of the class can't you wait?" "Come I want to show you something." The lady cast an irresistible smile and instantly her dimples got much pronounced leaving the young man gasping for breath. The lady opened her right arm immediately the young man inserted his left arm, and the two walked toward the library.

"Are you trying to get me into trouble with the teacher?" asked the young man not expecting an answer.

"Let's go. You worry too much about trivial things. Where is my kiss?"

"What?"

"Kiss me, here."

Fervently requested the lady pointing on her left dimple and then the right dimple then the forehead and then the lips. The young man smiled and quickly planted kisses on the dimples, the forehead, and the lips. The couple strolled toward the library with clasped hands. Later the couple entered the library.

"Waal the library is nearly empty."
"Exactly, now you see why I asked you to come with me now rather than later?" The lady quickly grabbed the young man's arm and walked toward the quieter section of the library. She passionately gazed at him with a fervent desire to be with him. Fervidly excited her eyes glittering. She looked at him and smiled infectiously making her dimples to be much pronounced. He reciprocated and passionately gazed at her too.

"Listen I will go first then you quickly come and find me. Okay?"

"You brought me here to play hide and seek. Are you sure?"

"Listen this is not a game. Quickly come and find me. Okay?"

Soon after the young lady vanished. Surprised, and a bit confused the young man stood there for a while bewildered and pondering what all this was about before going after the lady proceeding cautiously looking everywhere. The female librarian left her office until she reached a small corridor in the library leading to a huge big closed door. Midway she instantly stopped and listened before walking toward the room with a big door. She stopped again as she heard a whispering voice.

Stealthily she crept toward where the whispering voice was coming from. A quick glimpse further down the corridor revealed a young lady standing against the wall. Shocked and surprised she stopped and briefly peeped around. Stealthily she inched forward before stopping again and scanning the area. Another whispering voice from this lady sends the female librarian panicking, and this startled her even further.

"Kiss me."

Passionately whispered the lady in the corner near the door. The female librarian inched forward further creeping stealthily and slowly only to find the lady with her blouse raised up and flashing her huge assets with her eyes closed.

"I said kiss me." Passionately implored the lady with a fervidly sweet soft yet raised voice.

"What do you think you are doing?" Quizzed the female librarian with a raised voice. The lady startled, quickly opened her eyes, and pulled down her blouse and sprinted away. Nicodem suddenly appeared breathing very fast.

"What happened? You look like you have seen a ghost."

"Where were you? I told you to find me as quickly as possible. Why don't you listen to me?" The female librarian suddenly appeared as Nicodem was about to ask a question.

"This is a library; do you know that? Not some nesting cabin. Behave like other pupils. Why can't you go to the gardens?" Nicodem placed his arms around Ewa. "What is she talking about?" asked Nicodem surprised and curious. Saddened and with a sulking face, Ewa gave Nicodem a bleak look.

"Nico show me that you really love me. You are going to lose me. Be the first to find me. Look today someone found me first. I can't repeat what I did. Pay attention, will you? Oh my God surely you are going to lose me," she broodingly looked at him.

"You are not listening to me Nicodem. Someone could have taken me. Look at me. This is not a game. Pay attention and act quickly, run come and find me."

The librarian woman moved close to them pointing her finger at them.

"Silence and no more stupid games in here or you two you will find yourself outside the library. You heard me?"

"Excuse me? We haven't done anything wrong, in fact, we have a right to be in here. If you would excuse us?" The woman frowned and leaned forward.

"Only if you are using it for academic purposes and not flashing your private parts in here."

Nicodem looked surprised and fumed at the woman.

"What are you talking about? Who would do such a thing?" The woman looked upset and with wide-opened eyes pointing with her head too pointed at Ewa. Nicodem looked surprised and in disbelief leaned forward close to Ewa.

"Really? Is that true? I don't believe her." Seemingly embarrassed and looking away replied Ewa.

"Meant for you but too late now it's gone." Nicodem hugged Ewa, and the couple stood there for a while in each other's arms. "Really. I thought this is a game. Are you...?" Ewa interrupted.

"Surely you will lose me and never see me again. Show that you really want me. That you love me."

The female librarian coughed and looked at the couple.

"We are okay leave us," requested Nicodem.

"Behave or you will find yourselves outside," advised the assistant librarian before disappearing. Nicodem held Ewa's shoulders.

"What is all this about?"

Ewa gave Nicodem a grave look. Nicodem had never seen Ewa that sad.

"Pay attention and find me first. I chose you. You should be happy."

"Pardon me I did not think you are into us that much. I thought you were after Billy." Ewa laughed sarcastically.

"Me Billy? Please! I don't like a man I compete for the mirror with after all if it's not just liking himself too much, I think he is crooked. No offense but just not my type. I fancy you. A real man, not like Billy. A man who wears soft lip balm. No!" "Really?"

"Prove that you really love me. That you want to be with me forever and be the first to find me. Someone might come and take me."

"Why can't you fight them?"

"It's not that simple you are not listening to me."

"What's this boob flashing thing about?" "I can't repeat now. Go to that female librarian and ask her what exactly happened then quickly come back and find me." Explained Ewa walking away from Nicodem.

"Is it not time to go back to the class?" "You worry about that stupid class when I am giving you an opportunity no one has ever had. By the time this will make sense to you it will be too late."

"Stop talking like that you start scaring me now."

"Oh, Nicodem you are going to lose me. You are in the dark. You have no idea what this is all about. Don't you have dreams?" Nicodem cast a slack-jawed look and briefly smiled.

"Honestly, not really. Even if I have when I wake up, I won't remember a thing." "Really?"

Nicodem nodded his head before asking a question.

"I am not following you. What are we supposed to dream about if I may ask?"

"I can see you have no idea. This is not a game you know. Prove that you really want to be with me and always be there for me. Be the first to find me always." Nicodem looked confused and lost.

"So, what happened? What did you dream about?" Ewa gave Nicodem a flirtatious look and smiled.

"I was with you. We kissed and after we kissed, it seemed I could see myself. It seemed like looking in the mirror. There were two of us and I could talk to myself." "Really that's so spooky."

"Tell me about it."

"So, what happened after that?"

"After that, my sister woke me up and believe me I had a go at her for waking me up. I later apologized and explained what was going on."

"So, what did she say?"

"She said eh you and that creepy?" Nicodem instantly wore a sulking sad face. "Is that what your sister thinks about me? Why?"

"She said that that first day we met you could not get your eyes off my chest."

"No. I mean they are lovely assets but..." Murmured Nicodem.

"Eh but what?"

Quizzed Ewa pulling her blouse down and cheekily looking at Nicodem before winking at him.

"Eh, what?"

She poked out the tip of her tongue pressed against her top lip and moved it left to right before raising her eyebrows once in a flash.

"I mean... that day I was miles away. Honestly, I used to have dreams myself about some gorgeous lady and that day when I first saw you, it all seemed unreal. I just couldn't explain it. I felt like I was dreaming. I could see the lady standing in front of me. For a minute or two I could not separate reality from dreams. It felt like I was in another world. That could explain why maybe your sister thought that I was staring at your lovely assets not that I don't want to. It's just because these dreams have been going on for some time so vivid that it used to worry me a lot."

"So, what happened to this lady?"

Nicodem cast a dreamy look and sighed heavily. "The dreams after some time just stopped but I am looking at the lady right now."

"I knew it. It's not a coincidence. But I don't understand why you don't believe me."

"I stopped believing."

"Let's go back." Insisted Ewa pulling Nicodem's hand.

"No. Tell me more about your dreams." Ewa giggled strolling in the isle.

"A minute ago, someone was pestering me to go back with him to the class and now what? You are funny you know." A cat crossed the road and slid through the opening in the fence to a mansion in one of the suburbs. It was a frosty night with a breeze outside shaking the tree leaves. It was dark too and the barking of a dog pierced through the

almost silent night. Only the bathroom light was on.
The cat ran across the car park under the big SUV
and disappeared around the corner. Soon it let out a
sudden noise and jumped into the air. Another cat
appeared from underneath the SUV and meowed.
The main bedroom light instantly came on and the
cats disappeared. In the main bedroom, Nicodem
woke up and sat on the bed. He rubbed his face and
squinted his eyes looking at the alarm clock on the
dressing-table. He groaned and pushed his hair
backward before standing up and putting on the
fluffy slippers. He walked toward the bathroom. A
half-naked woman changed position on the bed and
soon fell asleep. Nicodem entered the bathroom and
looked at himself in the mirror. He opened the tap
and dosed his face with water. He looked into the
bathroom mirror and after a few minutes, he
switched off the bathroom lights and went back into
the bedroom and slept. A white silk lace wriggled
and floated in the air dancing to the wind before
being pulled around a corner. Nicodem stopped and
looked as the last piece of the silk lace disappeared
around the corner. He smiled and ran toward the
corner smiling and what seemed to be in slow
motion. Ewa giggled as she headed toward the other
isle and Nicodem could hear her giggling. Nicodem
in no time was in the other aisle and Ewa was
almost near him in the other isle. "Come find me.
Hurry," flirtatiously shouted Ewa before
disappearing again leaving the silk lace floating in
the air before it suddenly disappeared around the
second corner of the library isle. Nicodem sprinted
after her. The hide and seek continued for some

time before Nicodem reached the last isle only to find the silk lace on the floor. He stopped and skillfully scanned the area and knelt. Slowly he picked up the silk lace and sniffed it holding it close to his face briefly closing his eyes. A soft whispering voice startled him. He picked up the silk lace and inched forward toward where the voice came. He crept forward until the end of the aisle before hearing a sexy sweet passionate voice.

"Kiss me."

Nicodem inched forward stealthily looking everywhere for Ewa. He soon turned the corner hoping to see Ewa but to his surprise, she was not there. He looked around and walked to the huge door nearby. He tried opening it, but the door was locked. He investigated the entire area but Ewa had vanished without a trace. There were two ways out he thought. Through the isle or through the big door. "Ewa! Ewa!" shouted Nicodem feeling confused and frightened.

"Where are you? Stop playing games."

A small fading voice whispered Nicodem's name. Hysterically he tried to open the huge door, but it was locked from the outside. "Find me. Find me."

"Ewa! Ewa! Where are you?" shouted Nicodem shaking the huge door.

"Darling. Darling, are you having a bad dream?"

Nicodem opened his eyes and looked around. He looked at Natasha sleeping next to him.

"Is it that dream again?"

Nicodem did not reply but instead covered his face with both his hands before exhaling air.

"The dreams are so vivid it's frightening." "Take a break and find the meaning of all this."

"Just a dream darling."

"Could be a tip of the iceberg."

"It was in high school more than a decade ago."

"Investigate this once and for all. Just resolve it and move on?"

A few weeks later Nicodem jumped into his SUV and drove down the road leaving his girlfriend standing outside the gate. Many questions were running in his mind. These dreams lately have given him sleepless nights. The scary part was that they were so vivid and at one point he felt like Ewa had laid her hand on his chest. This was disturbing for him. What could this mean? A call for help or what? What happened to Ewa after high school? No one knew what befallen her. He had tried in vain to find her. For years he had ignored these dreams. A quick break was appealing. He acknowledged the need to break away from the monotonous routine lifestyle he had now become accustomed to. This was a break he needed the most. He had forgotten to enjoy life. He craved for the long journey back to his hometown. Honestly, the dreams were just an excuse. The truth is that in him there was still that feeling of reliving the old days where he cared less for money, jobs and all these things that seemed to have defined him lately. He had missed his old friends and the sense of not worrying about stupid material things. Freedom meant a lot to him. This was fundamental and of paramount importance. The chores of daily lives had bogged him down the worst thing he disliked. If it wasn't for Natasha surely his dream was to travel the world enjoying what life has to offer but Natasha being pregnant had meant going back to the drawing board. It was still freezing but much better than the previous days. For a while he had forgotten all about Ewa and the strange dreams he had been having. He remembered the first day he met Ewa. Surely it was surreal until now he still remembered pinching himself. What were the odds of something like this happening? This was out of this world even though he had been spot-on in the past. He remembered her smile and her voice. What might have happened to her. The dreams had been so vivid and frightening lately. He was happy. At last he was going to put this behind him. Nicodem quickly looked on the dashboard and played the Carolinadeivid song Seductive Beauty Back then I wanted to dance with her all night I wanted her all to myself Yes one evening, one lovely evening We decided to dance too much Then it happened. We kissed girl It was seductively sexy and so romantic. The SUV sped on the freezing tarmac road heading back to California. After a two-hour drive Nicodem arrived back in his home city all along his mind was running wild trying to imagine and predict what he was going to discover. All along he had left the Seductive Beauty song on repeat and honestly, he had not counted how many times the song had played but one thing that was for sure was that it had left an imprint in his brain that even after switching off the MP3 player he could still hear the song playing in his head. Surely not just another song and addictive too. This was part of the mystery that had given him sleepless nights. Meeting Ewa was such a strange experience especially after the dreams he had had in the past and now this. A strange feeling struck him. He stopped and cast a grave look. Had something bad happened to her. How strange enough that no one had seen her or heard anything about her after high school. He had met or heard something about most of the people he had known during high school. Strange enough she had vanished without a trace. The first place to visit as he had planned was the old school especially the library where it all started. A decade had gone without setting foot back here. This was his past and him being him he disliked dwelling on the past. He believed the past was the past. A means to prepare him for the future. His aims and goals were to experience the future as much as he can. Somehow nature had a different plan. The whole Ewa saga had seen him back again to his hometown. Excited and with grand expectations he entered the road the high school once was. Quickly he looked around to see if he can identify anything that could jog up his memory. Shocked and surprised the whole area had been changed and redeveloped. The small houses that once lined the road to the school had disappeared and had been replaced by huge mansions. The road had been redone with a lot of landscape surrounding it. After driving for a while, he stopped the car and smiled. At last he had seen one of the landscapes he recognized. Surely, he was in the right place. It seemed everything else had either been removed or changed apart from one landscape, a huge statue of one of the Greek goddesses. This brought about a lot of strange feelings. He remembered Ewa like yesterday. Briefly he smiled before casting a downcast look. What had happened to her? Only one way to find out. He drove forward heading to the old high school. The SUV stopped after a while and Nicodem cursed as he looked outside. "What happened to the school?" He asked himself with an astonished face. He jumped out of the SUV and stood outside. In front of him was a huge building. To his shock, it was the same place the library and school once stood. He remembered how this place once was. This time the place was different. The huge building was well protected with huge gates surrounding it. He walked toward the gate and as he reached the gate, the camera on the gate pillar instantly pointed at him.

"How can I help you?" asked someone through the PA system at the gate. Nicodem wore an absent look.

"Eh, what happened to the school?"

"What school? This is private property." Nicodem stood at the gate looking around. The voice on the gate PA system soon cuts off, and the camera turned away from him. "I would like to ask you a few questions," declared Nicodem pressing the PA system. The silence that followed was broken by a cracking voice.

"What is this about? Who do you want to see? Do you have an appointment?"

"Not really? I am looking for someone?" Silence broke out and later the huge gates opened. Hesitantly Nicodem walked inside and straight to the door. The doors opened instantly, and a woman sitting at the front desk smiled.

"What can I do for you?"

At first, Nicodem murmured some words.

"I am looking for a friend. I don't know where to start. This used to be the school?" He looked around and smiled.

"A long time ago before we acquired the land. Yes."

"I need access to the area once the library. Please."

"I am afraid not. It does not open to the public, its

private property now."

That afternoon Nicodem visited his former neighborhood. A few days later an SUV was seen parked outside the huge building. Later that evening a man entered the building carrying a bag. He rang the bell and after a while, the gates opened, and he entered the building. Nicodem opened his eyes after hearing Ewa's voice. He scanned the area and realized that he was in the library. He ran in the isle chasing after Ewa. Around the corner and into the other aisle and to his surprise she had disappeared.

"Ewa! Ewa! Where are you?"

He heard a whispering voice afterward.

"Kiss me. Kiss me."

Nicodem woke up scared and frightened that he banged his head in the air duct he was hiding in. For some strange reason he had felt someone touching his chest and a strange feeling had gripped him. As he raised his head up, he heard a faded whisper.

"Kiss me. Kiss me."

He crawled in the direction where the whisper came. The metal-air duct was freezing. Hours had passed by whilst still in the air duct. He realized he was in the new building where the school once stood. The metal-air duct was freezing as the building was now empty and all the heating systems possibly turned off. He crawled until he fell in one of the rooms through the loose cubed air fan. He fell onto the floor before getting up. As he got up, he had a quick flashback. In his flashback, he was in the library of the school. He looked around. Though the room looked different a small passage caught his eye and instantly a strange feeling struck him. Somehow, he realized that he had been there before. Slowly he walked toward the small passage and into the corridor. Another flashback. He remembered the time he went looking for Ewa. It seemed this was the same passage. At the end of the passage, the sight of a big door caused his heartbeat to beat fast. The door resembled the door he had seen before. Shocked and surprised he saw a statute of a lady next to the door exactly in the position that the assistant librarian had told him that she saw Ewa standing. The statute was that of a naked female holding her assets.

"What are the chances?"

Whispered Nicodem to himself. This was more than a coincidence. What was going on? In his head, so many questions ran in and out. Curious and fascinated he looked around and walked toward the huge door, but the door was closed. He stood there and instantly he had a flashback the time he was with Ewa. He remembered talking to the assistant librarian and whispered loud enough what the lady had told him.
"Kiss me."
Instantly an automated voice startled him.

"Correct magic word but wrong Geo-locational position."

"What?"

Nicodem looked around and tried to piece things together. He walked toward the statue of the naked lady. He stood there for a while before leaning forward to kiss the statue with his eyes closed. To his surprise, nothing happened, but he felt like some blue light had shown over his closed eyes. He tried again this time with his eyes opened. As soon as he had kissed the statue a blue ray of light flashed from the statue's eyes and instantly an automated voice sounded on the PA system 'Confirmation of initial registration. Please proceed to the door.' Instantly Nicodem walked to the door and as he approached, the doors opened. Central was a glass cabinet. A big mirror hung from the ceiling. Another cabinet stood against the wall. He looked around confused. He felt like he was dreaming. Was this for real? What was going on? He walked to the big screen embedded in the walls. He remembered talking to Ewa.

"Kiss me."

He repeated what Ewa had said to the assistant librarian and instantly an automated voice message came out of the wall screen.

"Incorrect magical word."

Nicodem looked surprised.

"Magic words. Ha?"

"Find me. Ewa."

"Incorrect magic word."

Nicodem tried to remember what Ewa had told him.

"Find me first. Be the first to find me."

The cabinet in the middle of the room opened up instantly and slowly a small golden box was lifted up. The box rotated clockwise in the middle of the room. Nicodem walked toward the box his heartbeat raised. Was this a game of some kind? Was he dreaming was this for real? Natasha lay on the bed after Nicodem had left. She remembered seeing a note in Nicodem's trousers with a telephone number. She had tried to call the number, but the cell phone was switched off. A lot of questions were popping up in her head. A recent program on television had made her jealous and not trusting. The ten signs that your partner is cheating on you had unsettled her since the last time she watched the program. Nicodem had been behaving strangely for the past months she recalled. All these sleepless nights, could it be that he was cheating on her? The intimacy between them had died. Nicodem was a strong man he rarely showed feelings but with her he was different. She knew he cared. He was passionate and romantic but that had died. For the past months it was either his work or these strange dreams. Every day, it was about this Ewa, these dreams or his work. He had lost that loving feeling. They rarely made love and if they did, it was a rushed thing. She had missed the romantic cuddles, the kissing and all that. Could he be cheating on her? This was the worst thing she thought could happen to her. Nicodem rarely talked about his past. It was only a few months ago when the nightmares started that she realized she knew little about the man she called her boyfriend. She realized Nicodem had a past flame. Was he still in love with this woman? Why now? This was the best time of her life. She had found the man of her dreams, an excellent job, a great house I mean everything was going according to her wishes until the last few months. Quickly she got up from the bed and opened the wardrobe. She took out Nicodem's briefcase and his laptop. She searched in the briefcase after struggling to open the lock. She searched inside but there was nothing in the form of pictures or addresses or telephone numbers. She searched through the laptop and there was nothing, no clues or anything. After a while, she searched for a file with the name Ewa. The laptop initially returned the 'no items match your search.' results. She looked at the laptop and decide to search in other drives. The search went on for a while. She looked again at the laptop and searched through Nicodem's folders and books and documents but there was nothing. It was when she was busy looking in the briefcase that a beep went off. Quickly she looked at the laptop and there was a hidden folder that matched her search. Her heartbeat skyrocketed, and she quickly checked the folder. The folder contained a picture of a small handwritten note.

"Kiss me. Find me. Yours Ewa Lenkostov." She felt her world falling apart. This guy was still in love with his past flame. Was he cheating on her? She felt upset for a while. Could they be making love right now? She quickly searched for any clues about the whereabouts of this Ewa Lenkostov. She searched for the phone directory and dialed every one of them. After a while, it seemed none of them matched this woman her boyfriend had been talking about lately. Surely, they must be of the same age or close age. The women in the directory were either too old or too young to have known Nicodem. She searched all local hospitals and registry offices. No record of this Ewa Lenkostov. She picked up the phone and called her boyfriend. She rang her boyfriend, but the phone rang and got diverted to voice-mail. She rang again and Nicodem answered, but he sounded weird as he started whispering. "I can't talk right now can I call you later." Soon afterward the phone call ended. Surprised and disappointed Natasha dialed Nicodem again.

"I can't talk right now. What is it darling?" whispering and with a very discreet voice answered Nicodem.

"What's going on? This Ewa did she tell you where she came from? Was she born in Cali?"

"I don't know really but definite she was not local. She said that she transferred from New York. Call you later," soon afterward Nicodem ended the call. Natasha searched for an Ewa Lenkostov in New York. She phoned all hospitals and educational facilities. There was no record of Ewa anywhere which matched the person she was looking for. Natasha picked up the phone and dialed Nicodem.

"Like I said I can't talk right now."

"Why are you whispering? Who is there with you?"

"What is it?"

"This Ewa where was she born?"

"Eh. I think she said in New York."

Natasha ended the call without waiting for Nicodem to say anything. She checked New York hospitals and dialed the number.

"Birth registrar please."

"Hold the line."

Music played in the background as she waited on the line. A moment passed before someone answered back.

"How can I help you?"

"I am looking for an Ewa Lenkostov. I think she is between 30 and 36 years old. Can you check birth records of anyone by that name?"

"Can I have your cell phone number I will get back to you?"

"Sure."

In a huge building, Nicodem stood in the middle of

the room. In front of him was a small golden box rotating clockwise. The room was very huge. Screens were mounted on the walls. An automated voice from the screen startled him.

"What is the magic word?"

"Magic word?"

Repeated Nicodem loudly that another automated voice sends him into a panic.

"Incorrect magic word."

Nicodem stood there in front of the box trying to remember everything. He remembered being in the library with Ewa. "Sister!"

He shouted and waited impatiently. "Incorrect magic word."

"Find me."

"Incorrect magic word."

"Kiss me."

"Incorrect magic word."

He remembered Ewa saying that she could see herself as if she was looking in the mirror.

"Clone,"

"Mirror,"

"Double,"

"Incorrect magic words."

He stood there trying to think what the magic word could be.

"Hide and seek."

Suddenly the golden box stopped rotating, and the box opened. With his heartbeat beating very fast he looked inside the box. He took the contents of the box and quickly left the building into his SUV and drove off. He took out his cell phone and dialed Natasha. The phone rang and instantly Natasha picked up and quickly asked a question.

"Was she born there?"

"Who are you talking about?"

Asked Nicodem.

"Sorry. It's you for a while I was dozing off. Nothing important, how are you? Did you find her?" asked Natasha.

"Listen, Nat, I am going to Latvia I have got a lead."

"Latvia? When will you be back?"

"I can't say for sure, but I will ring you when I arrive okay."

Soon afterward the line died. Natasha looked worried but at least settled. Nicodem wasn't cheating on her. This Ewa was still missing. The cell phone was still in her hand when the phone rang. She quickly looked at the number, it was a New York code.

"Hello."

"Yes. I can't talk over the phone. This is my address at the hospital."

The line soon went dead. Natasha quickly searched her purse and wrote the address down in her diary and left the mansion into her car and drove off. At San Francisco Airport she boarded a plane and headed to New York. A lot of questions were popping in her head, with a lot of expectations and curiosity she headed to the hospital's registrar office. On arrival, a man in his late fifties opened the door. "Please sit down," said the registrar pointing at the chair in front of him. Natasha sat down looking at the files on top of the office desk. The registrar sat down and wore his reading glasses before sighing and sitting comfortably in his chair.

"Yes, Sir. Was she born here?"

The registrar took the time to reply. He removed his reading glasses.

"Yes, but also died here. What is this about?" Natasha looked lost and confused. "Is there another Ewa Lenkostov? There must be a mistake. Surely not the person I am looking for?"

"The only Ewa Lenkostov. She could be 33 years old this year if she had lived."

"What do you mean she died here young?" "Yes. In fact, they were twins both died here as infants." Natasha stood up and walked toward the door.

"Wrong person. The person I am looking for went to school with my boyfriend. Are you sure this is the only Ewa born here?" "To the best of my knowledge yes." Natasha left the hospital with more questions than answers. She searched the local offices, schools, and registration offices but there was no record of a one Ewa Lenkostov. Nicodem after some hours he was in Riga, Latvia. It was getting dark; he checked into a hotel and rang his girlfriend Natasha. They spoke for hours before he went to bed. The following day he headed to the city's statue of liberty. He looked around the statute admiring the work of art when suddenly a whispering voice caught his attention. A quick glance revealed a lady standing in the park near the statue. The woman stood there staring back at him.

"Ewa!"

He looked surprised and excited and instantly ran after the lady. The woman wore a white lace covering her head and part of her face and most of her body. As soon as she had seen Nicodem running toward her, she sped off as fast as she can. His heartbeat beating very fast he remembered the first time they played hide and seek. He had lost. He threw a quick glance and chased after the woman. Across the park and straight into the big building located a few meters away from the park in which the woman vanished. Nicodem entered the building and looked around. He ran from corridor to corridor until he was very tired. He stopped to take a breath and looked in front of him. A silk lace floated in front of him.

"Ewa! Ewa! Wait for me." He sped toward the other end and in the direction the woman had gone. This led to the stairs going upward. A quick scan revealed a woman on the top balcony. He sprinted after her.

"Ewa! Wait."

The woman laughed before disappearing into the conference room above. Breathing heavily, Nicodem reached the top floor and looked everywhere, underneath tables and in every other room.

"Kiss me."

A whispering voice sliced the otherwise silent conference room. Nicodem rushed to the closed door. He pushed the door and saw the lady on the balcony.

"Ewa! No!"

Shouted Nicodem running to grab the woman who was about to jump.

"No! Wait! Ewa!"

The woman smiled and removed the lace covering her face.

"Ewa. It's me Nicodem."

The woman smiled showing her dimples but somehow covered her chest.

"Don't jump. Please. Stay with me. Wait." The woman looked down the balcony. The woman peeped down as if to jump.

"Wait. Please talk to me. Please stay." Pleaded Nicodem urging forward close to the lady.

"One more step and I will jump."

Nicodem stood still.

"Okay. I wait here. Talk to me. What is this about? You seem not to recognize me. It's me Nicodem.

Ewa please."

"Who is Ewa? I am not Ewa."

"What happened to you? It's me Nicodem." "I am Natasha. Natasha Lenkostov."

"Who? What happened to you?"

"Do you know Ewa? Ewa Lenkostov?"

"No. Should I?"

"Ewa had a sister but her name was Victoria. They were not twins as far as I know."

"I don't know Ewa. Like I said I am Natasha. If you would excuse me, I better be going home."

Nicodem cast a brooding face.

"What do you mean home? Seems you want to jump. You will die." Silently the lady gave a quick glimpse looking down the balcony.

"Okay. Okay. Talk to me. Where is home?" The woman squinted her eyes and threw a curious look at Nicodem.

"22 Florentine street New York. USA." Nicodem looked astonished but also confused, surely, he had heard that address before. He clearly remembered Ewa mentioning that address before.

"Do you know Ewa? Surely somehow you must be sisters. The resemblance is astonishing. I live in the USA too. I can take you there. Come let's go." The lady looked at Nicodem and smiled.

"Kiss me."

She whispered fervidly and closed her eyes. For a minute Nicodem thought that he was dreaming. It was so scary and confusing that he just stood there speechless. He couldn't move his legs even if he wanted to. Somehow it seemed like ages but only a few seconds had elapsed. "Kiss me."

"Ewa! Stop playing games."

She opened her eyes and cast an expressionless look at Nicodem. Instantly she slipped down leaving Nicodem speechless. It happened so fast but to him, everything appeared in slow motion. A quick dash after her, left him holding the lady's veil. The lady had jumped and vanished.

"No! Ewa! No!"

Shouted Nicodem before he ran downstairs through the double doors and outside the glass doors and into the pavement.

"Ewa! Ewa!"

"Kiss me."

A whispering voice startled him from the other side he quickly looked in that direction, but the lady had gone. Natasha was about to go back to California after her visit to New York looking for Ewa Lenkostov when her cell phone rang with a Latvian number. There was a moment of silence.

"I found Ewa's sister or twin I am not sure."

"Darling, did you say, twin? I am in New York right now. I tried to find this Ewa too."

"Really? Can you go to 22 Florentine street, New York and see what you can find?"

The line soon died and without wasting time Natasha headed to the address. This was a quiet neighborhood probably the poshest part of the city. The streets were quiet and deserted. The houses here were very huge with large gardens. In a rented car Natasha headed to the given address. Soon afterward she parked the car and waited in the car. She gathered her nerves and got out of the car into the yard of the house before a huge dog came running and wriggled itself on her. Instantly a woman appeared from the house.

"Don't worry. It's just a friendly dog." Natasha caressed the dog's head.

"Such a lovely dog." Said Natasha.

"Keeps me company. The house is too big alone."
The two women exchanged greetings and soon they
entered the house. "Tea or coffee?"

"Coffee please no sugar."

Moments later the woman returned with a tray with
cups of coffee.

"Beautiful house and such a quiet neighborhood."

"It's a lovely area the best place to raise kids." "So, I
suppose you have older kids?" The woman did not
reply but instead slowly sipped her coffee.

"Do you have any kids?"

"Me and Delaney were very blessed with our girls
only for them to be taken away from us."

"Very sorry to hear that," said Natasha putting
down her coffee cup.

"Ewa, Natasha, are they your kids?"

The woman looked sad.

"What is this regarding?"

She asked looking at Natasha.

"It's a long story but they are my boyfriend's
friends."

Silently the woman entered the lounge area and brought a picture frame. She sat down on the kitchen chair. Natasha stretched her hand and quickly looked at the picture. It was the picture of two twins very young probably three days old.

"Ewa and Natasha. My girls."

"Where are they now?"

Interrogated Natasha staring at the picture.

"Both taken away from us. My girls. Passed away together as infants." Natasha looked lost and confused.

"You mean these are Ewa and Natasha who died. Did you have other kids after?"

There was a moment of silence.

"After that tragic day, we never conceived again. We were very upset. They just died in their sleep at the same time."

"Ewa and Natasha Lenkostov?"

"Correct."

"If they died in infancy how come Nicodem said he went to school with them. How come he gave me this address and how did he know about these girls if they were dead."

"Who is Nicodem?" asked the woman. Natasha was busy brainstorming trying to come up with a logical explanation. Quickly she picked up the cell phone and called Nicodem.

"Come home, darling. Take the next flight home okay. Promise you come straight away."

"What did you find out?"

"Wrong address. Come, home, will you?" There was a moment of silence.

"Please come home I miss you. You have been gone for days now. Please come home."

Nicodem sighed heavily before putting the phone down. What is happening to my man? Is he hallucinating? Is it because of too much work? Maybe he needed a break that could explain why he is making up things. These were the thoughts running in Natasha's mind as she headed back home. That could explain the absence of Ewa's records. Could he have suffered a breakdown of some sort? Natasha even started to doubt that these ladies ever existed. Was Nicodem fantasizing about this woman? Unfortunately, the school no longer existed, and she knew very few people from Nicodem's school. The next day she headed to Nicodem's doctor. Nicodem returned home, and the two spent the night together in each other's arms. It was the following morning that Natasha raised the issue with Nicodem. "Darling if you like we can take a vacation just you and me. Maybe get away from all this. What do you say?"

"I just returned, and I am kind of busy. I was gone for days."

"Did you find anything in New York? Maybe I should go there myself."

Natasha looked worried and sad. She hugged Nicodem for a while.

"Darling you are hallucinating. These ladies are just in your head. I met Ewa's mum they both died in infancy. They were twins, yes, but both died many years ago." Nicodem cast a dark face at Natasha.

"You don't believe me?"

"Darling I searched everywhere for this Ewa and she does not exist. Maybe you should see your doctor." Nicodem sat down on the bed.

"See, you have been working very hard. Sometimes the brain creates these fantasies when you are stressed up. You see, you don't have any idea where this Ewa is. You have nothing that is tangible. Anyone from high school who can confirm that this woman existed?"

Nicodem got up and looked at his laptop and

retrieved some numbers and dialed. All the numbers were no longer in use. The school was no longer there. He remembered the lecturer. He searched on the Internet only to find out that the lecturer had already died.

"Billy! Surely Billy knew this lady," said Nicodem going through his laptop. The phone rang, and a female answered the phone.

"Billy? Where is Billy? Can I speak to Billy?"

"Are you related to Billy?"

"You can say that he was my friend in high school."

"I am afraid that he died a few weeks ago."
Nicodem looked surprised and lost.

"What did he say?" asked Natasha. Nicodem sat down with the phone in his hand.

"I can't believe this. Billy is dead." Natasha looked at Nicodem and sat next to him before hugging him. Quickly Natasha rushed out of the bedroom and into the lounge area and quickly came back upstairs with her handbag. She took out her cell phone.

"I have something to show you. Look at this."
Nicodem looked at the image on Natasha's cell phone.

"Where did you get this? Who gave you this

picture?"

"Do you know them, darling? Is that Ewa and Natasha?"

"What is going on?"

A lady wearing a silk see-through nightdress with barefoot ran out from the house at night giggling past the veranda into the garden. It appeared as if in slow motion, with her hair and dress floating into the air. Instantly a man appeared at the door before running onto the pavement then into the garden. The lady looked backward while still running and smiled signaling to the man asking him to follow her. Her hair floated in the air before she vanished into the nearby garden.

"Wait for Ewa. Wait!" Shouted the man before sprinting after her and as soon as he reached the garden he looked around and it appeared that he was standing in front of a huge lake. He looked around surprised and shocked. Instantly he jumped into the lake and dived deep down looking around shouting the woman's name. The screeching of car tires outside sends Natasha into a panic.

"Nicodem, Nicodem, wake up. There is someone outside Nicodem."

Nicodem woke up disoriented. Car lights shone through the bedroom window before another screeching sound was heard. Nicodem opened the bedside drawer and took out his gun and quickly ducked next to the window before peeping outside. "Damn! Get up. Take the car keys. Hurry back door garage. Hurry."

A haunted face he wore said it all, danger! Natasha without hesitation grabbed her coat and the car keys and disappeared leaving Nicodem peeping outside. Seconds later Nicodem rushed downstairs and into the kitchen straight into the garage before feeling a sharp pain on his forehead. A black BMW X5 cruised at high speed past a car driven by an old woman leaving her shaken as she drove out of the way just a few seconds before the BMW kissed the back of her car. The woman parked on the roadside for a while shaken and scared before she resumed her journey. Another woman from the nearby building near the city center looked outside witnessing every minute of the incident.

"Any thoughts on what's going on with Nico?"

Quizzed the woman sat on the couch. She appeared to be in her early thirties with a huge volume of hair that made her head look huge. The woman gazed outside witnessing the near-miss before casting a slack-jawed face for a while. For a while, she acted as if she had not heard the question. She stood there glancing outside. "Janet, I wish to know what to believe. So many questions remain unanswered."

"But he is your boyfriend if you don't believe him then who will?" Natasha looked outside the window for a while.

"He never talked about his high school years, the only person he talked about is Billy." She looked at Janet with a sad face, numb and distraught.

"So, what did this Billy say?"

"Billy died a few weeks ago." Silence sliced through the room as the women searched for clues.

"What about the school?"

"Closed and replaced by a modern huge building."

"Surely there must be someone who knew her don't you think?"

"I have a lead but it's not that promising." "What do you mean?"

"The woman has witnessed many birthdays not sure if her memory serves her right." Later that day a land rover discovery parked outside a huge building. Side by side the women entered the nursing home. A woman sat inside the glass veranda swinging looking toward the beautiful garden. The two women sat next to her on both sides.

"What a night. It seemed colder here shouldn't you be inside with the others?" The old woman cast a Mona Lisa smile and looked unconcerned by the freezing weather.

"Strangely, for years I woke up early in the morning bracing this weather and going to work. I loved it. It's a shame they closed that school. I still could be there you know?"

"So, what happened?"

"One day we just heard that the land was acquired for development. That was that." Silence sliced through as the women threw each other a quick glance. Natasha opened her bag and took out a picture for a while and held onto it before handing it to the woman.

"They have come and gone over the years. You meet all kinds of pupils. In the end, they all look alike to me." Natasha opened her bag and took out Nicodem's old school days photo and gave it to the old woman. The photo was from one of the library magazines. Squinting the woman held the picture close. Another look then she gave the photo back to Natasha.

"Who is that supposed to be?"

The women threw each other a quick glance before Natasha spoke to her.

"We heard stories that you took a couple to the headmaster's office complaining that they were misbehaving in the library." The woman's face lit, and she stretched her hand reaching out for the photo. She looked at the photo again and smiled.

"Is that him? Are they married now? Are you that silly girl?"

Quizzed the woman touching Natasha's face. Natasha smiled and looked at Janet. "You still remember her?"

Inquired Janet.

"Is that you? What happened? Where is he?"

"So, the story is true? What do you remember about this woman?"

The old woman cast a radiant face and smiled. She squinted at the picture again. She wore a dreamy face before smiling again and staring at Natasha and Janet simultaneously.

"Until that morning I had not witnessed something like that before."

She cast a radiant smile.

"I thought she was mad, but I guess, if you are in love, they say you can do anything.

Young and foolish where the best then than the warmth and privacy of the library? I was so sure she would not finish her studies before she got pregnant. After thinking it over I decided to medley and help them." Silence broke out for a while. "Help them how?" asked Janet.

"Just imagine their parents paying such money to send them to school only for them spending time in the library at it like rabbits. Surely I had to do something." The women cast a straight-faced look at each other.

"What did you do?" The rattling of a low-flying helicopter startled the people as it hovered around the city. People in the cars below looked up through the windows as the helicopter lifted all kinds of dirt from the ground into the air. The nearby windows of the building shook and vibrated as it flew past turning left and up again into the air high until it reached the top of the longest building. It circled the tallest building before landing down. A couple smartly dressed up carrying briefcases got out and strolled toward a door before disappearing inside. In the conference room, a well-dressed man, wearing a white waistcoat and a badge tie got up and walked toward the large screen. He touched his cheeks with his left hand and stroked his tie with his right hand. A beeping sound from the screen startled him. He looked at the screen and quickly moved back to his seat and quickly punched the keyboard of his laptop. After a while, two flashing lights appeared on the screen. He quickly lifted his laptop and walked to the big screen. He stood there for some seconds before carrying back the laptop to his desk and took out his cell phone.

"Sir, there is something you should see. I am in the conference room."

Vicky entered the bank and looked at the photo on the desk and smiled. This was the best time for her. She looked at David in the photo on the desk and smiled. She looked at David in the photo standing behind her with his arms around her stomach. A sudden rush of strong craving feelings suffocated her putting her in a trance for a second or two. The sight of him with his strong arms around her waist made her soft bits tremble with passion. David was now the man of her dreams. She had everything she had wished for. She remembered that not so long ago all her friends were happy and that they teased her when she was lonely. She smiled at how quickly things had turned her way. A fantastic job, a house, a car and loads of cash. All this meant her dreams coming true. There was a great man in her life. The intimate sex session that morning made her drool uncontrollably. Any slight contact between her flesh left her paralyzed and unable to think. She walked toward the window in her huge office in one of the bank buildings. The view through the window was out of this world. This office was not just an office. This was part of the huge package to keep her with this bank after years of success. Everyone knew she was a workaholic, but the sudden appearance of this mystery man has turned her into one of the softest princesses around. Any knock at the door or the sudden ringing of her cell phone would send her into a trance. Her colleagues had recently noticed this dramatic change. In her building floor, there were two other investment managers who were under her, namely Tim and Mart. Mart looked through his office glass wall and saw Vicky smiling to herself standing at the window looking outside. For a while he got lost looking at her until Tim said something. "She is your boss mate forget about it. I know what is going on in your head," Mart blushed and tried to hide it.

"She has been an angel lately. A minute ago, she dragged out her silk dress between her butt cheeks. You know what that means?" Mart looked with a curious face. Tim casually looked at Vicky casting a sly face. Mart inched closer and whispered. "She has gone commando. I think she is gagging for it or she just can't get enough." "How can you tell just by looking at her?" "Experience mate. Experience. Look at the tell-tell signs. Silk dress, the smiles, and caressing herself. You should know all this."

"I am not a player like you. Married to one woman since my teens so honestly, this is out of my radar."

"OK watch this."

Mart stood up pushing his chair backward, wiped his lips downward, moisturized his fingertips before moistening his beard. He stroked his tie before leaving the office and knocked on Vicky's door and instantly opened the door without waiting for an answer. Vicky startled and instantly turned around to answer the door and before she knew it, the door opened wide instantaneously getting caught pulling the silk dress out from the groove between her butt cheeks. She looked embarrassed and shy.

"You look perfect lately, you are beaming with elegance just couldn't help?" Mart did not finish talking as they both heard Tim giggling in the next-door office. They both looked through the window and saw Tim who instantaneously pretended to be busy. "You two are you spying on me?"

"I know I might be out of tune here but hey, fancy going out for drinks or coffee sometime?"

"Mart, you have a girlfriend. I have a new man in my life. Thanks, but no thanks." Mart looked surprised and numb for a second or two.

"Since when, last time I checked you were, eh?"

"Eh if you don't mind, I am kind of busy," said Vicky smiling and strolling slowly like a model toward the other side of the office and smiled at Tim before pulling the rails closed. Mart all this time was looking at Vicky's perfect figure especially her assets. One thing was for sure Mart had never seen Vicky so happy. Soon afterward Mart closed the door without saying anything and stood outside Vicky's office.

"What are you still doing there? Get some work done for a change," she laughed and drew her chair and sat down. Moments later Vicky heard Mart opening the door of the office he shared with Tim instantly she heard Tim laughing uncontrollably.

"She is your boss man. All these months you said that she was not your type what has changed today?"

"Something about her. I cannot pinpoint what exactly but damn she is pressing every right point."

"I can hear you two. Get some work done before I drag you into my office," shouted Vicky. The two men threw a quick glance at each other and could hear Vicky giggling to herself in her office. The relationship between these three had recently changed. They were now closer together. The Vicky they knew was a workaholic this was a new Vicky, sexy and flirtatious. Mart realized that she had found real love. Love that gave one wing. A red BMW M8 cruised on the highway at a fast speed leaving behind drivers with envy. David, a well-built handsome man with dimples on his cheeks and chin and a million-dollar smile was driving the car. He had a very clean shave with short but voluminous hair wearing dark sunglasses. He looked quickly in the side mirror and looked at himself and brushed his hair backward before looking ahead. He took out a blue-tooth device and inserted the earpiece. The phone rang, and he smiled to himself. Instantly someone answered the phone.

"Hey Sweetie, I am heading to the gym can we meet

for lunch later?"

"Darling. I have been thinking about you I just can't seem to get enough of you."

"That sounds good. I can come over in a flash maybe lunch in your office?"

"Would love to darling. See you at 1 pm." Later a car parked outside the huge building in the city center and David got out, a well built and well-toned man leaving the onlookers admiring his physique. A beautiful brunette looked at him and with a soft sexy voice said hi to David. David looked at her as she passed by.

"Sorry I am already taken but you can come and watch me training."

The woman giggled and walked past pressing her breasts together. David smiled and shook his head before heading inside the gym building. He raised his hand at the sexy receptionist and headed inside. He took out his wrist mp3 player and selected the Carolinadeivid song Angels and hot lips and smiled to himself. After warming up he got down doing what he loved doing best. Everyone in the gym looked at him pumping iron to the Angel and hot lips song. Miles away Vicky felt like a teenager on heat. Every time she crossed her legs she felt being aroused. She looked at the time and it was 12 noon. Lunch was still one hour away. It wasn't the food that she looked forward to, no. It was the steamy session with her now-boyfriend. David was hot no doubt but all these years the men she found attractive were totally different. Men who had real power, financially and business-wise. She was attracted to successful businessmen. Men with same dreams as hers. This job had made her feel very successful and for the first time, she changed her priorities and values. Meeting David made her feel loved, young, carefree and sexy. Sessions with this hunk were mind-boggling. She felt like a teenager again. David was on her mind all morning. The desk clock showed the time as 12:30. A knock on the door startled her and hesitantly she answered the door.

"What is it?"

"I have some files that need your signature."

"Come in."

Tim walked in and sat down. Vicky signed the files as fast as she can and handed them back to Tim. Tim left the room and another knock on the door stopped Vicky doing what she was doing. Mart entered the office without waiting and handed the files to Vicky. Vicky looked at Mart and smiled then shook her head and quickly signed the files.

"Lunch?"

"Oh yeah sure but with my boyfriend, he will be here around 1 pm. Mart smiled and left the office.

Vicky worked as fast as she can as she looked forward to having lunch with David. She looked at the watch the time was now 12.55. A big smile on her face said it all. Honestly, she was hot and gagging for it. Every move and any slight friction between her legs kept senses elevated. Slowly she uncrossed her legs and spread them apart and the excitement was so unbearable that she stopped punching figures on the keyboard and instantly she slid her hand under the desk and pulled the silk dress toward her groin. Instantaneously she shivered as she instantly felt being aroused as the silk dress stroked her clitoris passing some static electric current through the hood. Immediately she closed her eyes and felt saliva oozing out from every part of her body. What's the hack? I might as well give myself one now. She thought out loud. Unconsciously she lifted her legs banging her knees on the underside of the table. She tilted her head onto her left shoulder and stroked her clitoris, pulling the hood so much that her clitoris soon became fully exposed turning into white as blood disappeared to the surrounding region which instantly turned red with blood. With her right hand, she caressed the ridges of her soft pussy and soon finds herself rubbing every part as fast as she can and instantly a strong sweet feeling oozed from the inside of her mouth that she started licking her inner side-cheeks. The feeling became so intense about to send her over the edge.

"I am going to come. I am going to come." She whispered to herself. This was it. The feelings were so intense. She just couldn't stop even if she wanted to. She stretched wide her legs and pulled very hard the skin surrounding her clitoris exposing it, even more, this time. Instantly a beep sound came out from her computer and instantaneously she felt like something jumped into her body. She felt an intensified strong feeling that elevated the arousal and straight away she felt like sneezing and climaxing while she stroked her clitoris faster and faster tilting her head to the left in ecstasy. This was it, she felt like exploding before she let out erotic moans followed by a wild ferocious orgasmic scream as she climaxed so hard, sneezing, and squirting at the same time and in a fraction of a second followed by what appeared to be a pained scream. She squirted so hard that she heard the squirt hitting the computer screen and some in the form of droplets splashing back onto her face. Watery mucus oozed out of her nose as well. 12:56 Tim and Mart were busy processing the last transactions just before lunch. In fact, this was everyone's busy time. Vicky had just logged on into the main system about to update the system when she decided to give herself an early orgasm. She looked at her watch and the time was 12:55, still logged in with four minutes to spare, she started pleasuring herself unable to control herself. In the other office next door Mart and Tim were busy working. Vicky had closed the window curtains after Mart and Tim were spying on her. Mart looked at Tim.

"The last transactions before lunch. I can't wait.

Honestly today I wanted to take Vicky out for lunch."

"So, what did she say?" Mart looked at Vicky's office, but the curtain rails were shut.

"She told me that her boyfriend was coming to pick her up."

"I think we should go early for lunch I don't want to sit here whilst they are fucking each other in there. After all, I don't want to see that guy." Mart immediately stood up and looked toward Vicky's office. Instantly an error message appeared on the screen and instantaneously the computer began the shutting down process.

"Eh, what are you doing I haven't finished making the last transactions before lunch?" Shouted Mart.

"What are you talking about?" asked Tim. Both their computers were automatically shutting down.

"I did not shut down the computer."

"Me either."

"What's going on?"

The men threw each other a quick glance. Something had happened somehow both were logged out of their accounts. Mart quickly went into the IT room and looked at the main network board.

His computer, Tim's and everyone's computer on their floor were all disconnected from the network. The network connectivity indicators had either turned to red or amber. Surprisingly there was only one network gateway still activated showing as strong green light. Only one green light visible. The rest were down. Mart thought that was strange and quickly left their office without saying anything. Mart stood outside Vicky's office door about to knock when he heard Vicky letting out an intense orgasmic-scream-like sound. The sound was very familiar. He stood there for a while and pressed his ears against Vicky's door.

"Is David here already?" Mart asked himself looking at his wristwatch, it was 12:57. Vicky and everyone for that matter never left early or invited anyone before 1 pm mainly because of these last five-minutes banking transactions before lunch. In the office, Vicky passed out. Mart had just left the office he shared with Tim after noticing the green light in Vicky's office was on when all network lights on their floor were either red or amber. Whilst outside Vicky's office Mart heard Vicky let out this loud sound. The sound was very familiar. He stopped at the door and listened pressing his ear against Vicky's office door. He had a quick flashback when his girlfriend had an intense orgasmic scream. This sound was unmistakably similar. Had David been there already? Were they making love? What frightened Mart was that the last scream he heard sounded like a scream of pain rather than that of pleasure. Confused he stood there outside Vicky's office. It happened in a few minutes, but it seemed like a long time. Mart knocked on Vicky's office door.

"Ah!"

Instantaneously Vicky let out another scream. This scream sounded like the being-scared or in-pain-scream. Mart remembered Vicky telling him that David was coming for lunch. Another knock and there was no answer.

"Vicky are you okay?"

Still no answer. Mart went back to the office he shared with Tim.

"Is she okay?"

"Not sure really? Is her boyfriend in already I thought that I heard her coming like hell? This guy must be good."

"Seemed the network had crashed. I can't even reboot it. You know what? I am starving I can't be asked we can call IT after lunch. Okay?" In Vicky's office, a lot was happening there. The seconds before she climaxed, she had felt like something had jumped into her body intensifying the arousal making her orgasm so hard that she squirted and sneezed simultaneously so hard that she had no control of her valves something she had never done before. Squirts and watery mucus from her vagina and nose spoiled everything, the chair, the table, the carpet, and the computer screen. She seemed to have blacked-out after climaxing for a few seconds. The knock on the door awoke her up. What happened after was still a mystery. Something so scary and confusing had happened to her leaving her numb. She heard Mart's knock on the door but when she opened her eyes, she couldn't see anything. It was that dark she couldn't see anything but to her, it seemed so weird because she knew for sure she had opened her eyes. That explained the second scream that seemed to have caused the second short blackout when she got scared and confused. What happened after that honestly, she had no clue. It felt like a long time though. David looked at his watch and it was 12:58 as he got out of the elevator and walked toward Vicky's office. A slight knock on the door and he was inside the office. Vicky seemed to have woken up instantly from a deep sleep. Scared and confused but very delighted to hear David's voice. She instantly opened her eyes.

"Oh, I can see!"

"Vicky, what's going on here?"

Interrogated David surprised. Mart heard a man's voice in Vicky's office and quickly walked toward the office pushing the door without even knocking.

"Oh my God."

Yelled Mart looking at Vicky. She had her knickers down to her knees. She looked shocked and scared but for some strange reason, she was not at all worried by the fact that her knickers were down to her knees. David gave Mart a quick glance. Mart gave Vicky a pained look. A feeling of jealousy and betrayal got into him. Mart quickly solved the puzzle the moment he gave the two a brief glimpse. He tried to remember whether he had knocked or not then realized that he was not supposed to be there. He felt embarrassed and quickly was about to leave when he felt David grabbing his collar. Vicky's office smelled female fluids there was no doubt she had just had an orgasm. The moment Vicky's boyfriend entered the office Vicky's eyes instantly opened delighted to see her boyfriend she looked at him but something else caught her attention. A message appeared on the screen in a flash and disappeared in a flash as well before the computer instantly started shutting down. Vicky looked even more shocked and surprised. A few seconds later Mart entered the office and the next time she looked at the screen the computer had already begun automatic shutdown. Tim checked his watch, and it was lunchtime. All the efforts to try to reboot the computer were in vain. Walking out of the office Tim saw Mart standing inside Vicky's office. He peeped inside.

"Oh my God. You guys. Mart, what are you doing in there? Leave them alone let's go for lunch." Tim pushed the door open and saw Vicky sitting in her seat. All the men looked at her. Something was wrong. Vicky cast a haunted look. The three men instantly felt what she was feeling. "Something happened," explained Vicky with a sad face.

"Oh yeah, we can see that."

Ridiculed Tim before bursting into laughter. Mart looked at Vicky. Something bad must have happened. To Mart, this was a different Vicky, fragile and weak. She looked so scared and confused and for some reason didn't even bother covering her private parts. David initially gave Vicky a sardonic look before wearing a sullen face. He had never seen Vicky this way.

"Pull up your knickers babes what's going on?"

Vicky acted like she had woken up from a trance, confused and disoriented. She quickly looked down and stood up pulling up her knickers.

"What's wrong with her she is acting as if she has suffered a breakdown." Mart looked worried normally this would be his favorite subject but for some reason, he looked lost and worried. Surely something terrible might have happened to Vicky. "What is wrong with you? You look like you have seen a ghost?" Back in the office, Vicky got up and tightly hugged her boyfriend for some time.

"I am scared please don't leave me. Let's go home."

"Isn't it lunchtime?"

"I know please take me home. Just take me home darling will you."

"OK, I guess we have to go home."

A white Lamborghini screeched its tires going via a bend in the road before speeding off. Driving was a 22 years old handsome young man. He looked next to him and activated the car phone system, pressed a button, and waited. The phone rang for a while before someone answered. "Your call, all set."

"Play the song."

Soon after the line went dead. The Lamborghini cruised in the surrounding suburbs before entering one of the mansions. The young man entered the mansion and downstairs into the studio. He rehearsed for some time before his phone started ringing. He ignored the phone and continued rehearsing for some time until the phone started ringing again. He left the studio.

"Played the song on air."

The young man looked haunted for a while. Immediately he went upstairs to his private study room. He pressed the button of the remote on the table and a screen suddenly appeared floating in the air. He stood there in front.

"Play song 3," the song by Carolinadeivid; The one

song, started playing in the background as a video played simultaneously. The young man looked closer.

"Pause."

Instantly the song and the video stopped playing.

"Zoom. 50%"

"Resume."

The music continued playing so as the video. The young man stood with an expressionless face. Another quick glance at the screen then he turned off everything and sat on his desk.

CHAPTER TWO

A private jet landed at a private runway before
coming to a halt. Immediately a man in his fifties
and a woman got off the plane. They entered the
limousine outside before they were chauffeured
away. The limousine arrived at one of the city
hotels and the pair headed to one of the suites. "You
worry too much for nothing. Relax let's enjoy life.
You seem so tense." The man cast a haunted face.
Immediately he briefly looked at the beautiful
woman in front of him. He put his arms around her
and kissed her.

"I told you. Take a break from all this. Wind down
and enjoy life. Life is not about the money you
know."

The man sat down and breathed heavily. The
woman followed him and sat on his lap.

"It's just money darling soon you will get more."

"You don't understand. I can spend more money no problem as long as I am making even more money I don't mind."

"What's your financial situation?"

"One of my companies isn't making any money. In fact, I am losing money every month." The woman gave the man a curious and interrogative look. She sat down.

"Is that the reason why you have been so tense lately."

"This company was my major income generator and for the past months I can't figure out why this has suddenly become an issue."

"All those people you pay salaries every month can't give you an answer?"

"Not that simple. Its factors beyond our control."

"Nothing beyond your control remember?" "That was then this is now."

"Viktor! Grab the bull by the horns. Nothing is beyond your control. You used to say that what happened? Where is that hungry man? You seem like a shadow of yourself. No excuses. No matter what it takes. I told you. I love flying, I love private jets and I like this lifestyle. Do something about this. You can't stop now. You worked hard all your life and lose that to what?" Viktor knew Elina had a point. Equally, he knew that a wind of change was on the horizon. His south coastal company had suffered losses in recent months. This was the major income generator. The past months had been tough. When you start losing money like this, surely it is a cause for great concern. Everything hinted to the need to take the bull by the horns. This was not the man he once was. He believed in an arduous yet smart work and rewards, but some unforeseeable force was on the horizon creaming away all his profits. It had gone so bad that he had started losing his own money. The south coastal company was his major source of revenue and over the years he had thrived. His business had thrived, and he had gained a lot of reputation and trust but that was about to change. In recent years there had been an influx of similar businesses to this coastal area and competition had meant dwindling revenues. The newcomers had provided cheaper versions at minimal cost. His market base was dwindling every month. He relied on trust and loyalty to the brand, but the cheaper versions had meant stiff competition. Somehow these newcomers had won the trust of his once trusted customers. He provided value though at soaring prices. He had believed that this would guarantee him an ever-growing customer base but somehow the new industries had proved to be a pain in the butt for him. Viktor looked lost for a while.

"Don't beat yourself up. Do something about this. I told you last time. Remember that time when they were voting? I told you that you have to be strong and do what no one else can do."

"I did my best."

"No, you did not."

"What do you mean?"

"You were in control you had power over other business owners. You were like God. I told you. Don't listen."

"They voted to put new laws. What was I supposed to do?"

"That time you controlled everyone was your best chance to foresee this and put new laws yourself."

"That would mean playing dirty tricks. I am a businessman. I have ethics."

"Ethics. You think ethics will solve anything?"

"There must be something that can be done to generate revenues. I can adjust and rebrand ourselves again."

"I love this lifestyle anything other surely I will leave you."

Viktor cast a sardonic face that seemed to say see if I care. Deep down he knew she had a point. He was losing money at an alarming rate. The influx of new businesses meant reduced income and stiff competition. He never thought that he would lose trust and loyalty over these new cheap industries. He had to do something, or the future was bleak. He had emphasized quality and had hoped that alone would see him through but a new force he reckoned was lurking around. Only he could correct that. A tall slim sexy lady with perfect curves and a smile to match strolled out of the city building walking as if she was on the catwalk. She cast a radiant face. Everyone looked at her with lust, envy and jealous. The lady was in her mid-20s wearing a suit and carrying an expensive purse. Far away a revving sound was heard that shifted the attention from this gorgeous lady to the sudden appearance of a white shining and mint Lamborghini. Everyone looked at the car as the loud music was coming out of the opened roof. The beautiful lady slightly annoyed by the sudden takeover of attention stopped and looked around before fixing her eyes on this Lamborghini as well. The car had parked a few feet away in front of her. A young man slid out of the car. Everyone looked astonished. Anita looked surprised as well she had expected a man in his late forties to jump out of the car. The young man looked unconcerned about Anita's presence as he quickly walked past her brushing against her causing her expensive purse to fall.

"Be careful with that. That's not borrowed

merchandise. I bought this you know?" said Anita sounding jealous and upset. "Excuse Moi, madam. I apologize but just to correct you neither did I borrow that sexy babe of mine. I bought it with my own money."

"Please. Someone gave you the keys to park the car and you as naughty as you are, you are driving it around."

"Oh, here we go again. You see, when God has blessed you with everything, good looks, plenty of money and an attitude to match you will always find skeptical people like you. People who will always question everything. I look young, in fact, I am young, but I earned all this I work hard I mean smarter. In fact, I don't see myself as young. I feel like a mature man you know."

Anita took a closer look at Joe looking everywhere even his private parts before quipping.

"Yeah right mature man my ass."

"Fancy spending some time with me maybe show you how mature I am?"

"Thanks, but no thanks. I am kind of busy myself."

"Sorry my name is Joe and you are?" "Anita. You know what. I will give you my number when you are free maybe call me." "Guess how many women throw their knickers at me let alone their phone numbers. Honestly, I am not going to call." "But I am not all those women."

"That's exactly what they all say. You know what? Come with me first later I will drive you around. I must do this first. Okay." The couple entered the nearby building and into the elevators all the way to the top level.

"Listen when we are inside don't talk just look at me and smile and nod your head. I will say you are my business partner. Don't let me down we just met, and I am trusting you. Something about you. I feel like we have known each other for a while. Okay." "Okay."

The pair threw each other a quick glance. "What is it that you do?"

"Oh my God, I thought you recognized me?" "Hello!"

"Surely you must have seen me on television or magazine somewhere." "Hmm. Not really."

"I am the best music producer around or you know my father? A music producer as well. The one? The ten rules?"

"Never heard of him."

The elevator door opened, and the couple entered the corridor and straight to a huge door that Joe struggled to open before Anita came to the rescue. As the door opened slowly Anita and Joe saw the inside of the office, one of the luxurious offices around. They entered in. Above was a glass ceiling, and the office had expensive sofas and chairs. Viktor was dressed to kill. Very smart in an expensive Italian suit. His hair shining and sleek with a clean shave. He had a dark blue suit with a blinding white shirt and a dark blue tie. He looked and smelled a billion dollars. Joe realized and acknowledged that he was no near this man. The way he talked dictated riches and authority. He was one of a kind or at least the best Joe had seen. Viktor strolled toward the window and gazed outside before requesting the couple to sit down. "How can I help you two?"

"No how can we help you?"

"Do I look like I need help?" Anita briefly glanced at Joe before wearing a Mona Lisa smile. There was a moment of silence.

"Sir, with all due respect I think you are heading for disaster unless you do something about this."

"I don't know what you are talking about." Joe stood up and walked toward the window and took a quick glimpse of the outside.

"Imagine you have worked hard all your life and established yourself as the ultimate tycoon over the years. Also, imagine the sudden ruthless wind of change. Imagine not able to make a profit for months from your most lucrative investment. You might not see it now, but the problem isn't getting any better. Every day new companies establish themselves and want a piece of your cake. In a few months, the entire cake is gone. You realize you still got other cakes but how long before the other cakes are gone too?" Viktor looked very uneasy. He started breathing heavily. He unfastened his tie and sat on the edge of the seat.

"All this information is private and confidential."

"That's how it is supposed to be but, in fact, it's out there if you really need it."

"What are you saying?" Joe looked outside for a while before walking back to his seat and sat down.

"The future is bleak. Imagine not making any profits? This is a fact in the near future."

"What do you want? Why are you frightening me? My men are taking care of this. I have the best in the field."

"With all due respect Sir. You had these men for the past months, but they seem not to do anything beneficial. I mean, as I see it, you will lose more at an alarming rate that you will be out of business in a flash."

"Young man I have more than five coastal

companies the highest income generators. Just because one is not doing well doesn't mean there is a crisis." Viktor stood up and walked toward the window and looked outside. Joe and Anita looked at each other.

"We looked at all the options we can't do anything. It's a free market these cheap products are eating away our profits."

"I know you have no other options but mine."

"What do you mean?"

"Joe stood up and walked toward the window near where Viktor stood.

"Sir the problem is not the competition, or the cheap products or mistakes by your business advisers. No." The silence broke out and Viktor looked at Joe with wide-opened asking eyes.

"So, what is it then Young-man?"

"First, I want $10 billion, $1billion now the rest after the job is done."

"Are you fucking crazy!" shouted Viktor. "$10 billion," whispered Anita louder enough that the two men looked at her. "Yes $10 billion."

"No way that's as much as is left. I am losing a lot of money."

"I know that's why I am here."

"$10billions. No chance." Joe walked very close to Viktor.

"Look I am here to make you filthy rich. I need someone who is a billionaire already for this to work otherwise I could have done it myself." "Why you need me for. I have established a reputation and I am not going to let anything change that."

"Why is it that there has never been a Trillionaire? When we have trillions in the entire world? Because man is hesitant, scared and focuses only on immediate needs. Look globally. Think globally. Why is it hard to acquire all these trillions to yourself? Mankind lacks courage and foresight. It takes a very strong heart to do this. Morally is it acceptable or not? Honestly it depends." Viktor looked at Joe and walked to his comfy sofa. Joe took out his laptop and played a video. The three watched the video. A woman left the department store with bags full of designer clothes and walked onto the pavement before a beeping sound caught her attention. She stopped and looked at her cell phone. She had just received a message. As soon as she had finished reading the message, she looked frightened and quickly she scanned the area. She looked near the car park and saw a man standing there looking at her. Instantly her heartbeat started beating very fast initially finding it hard to breathe. She started walking very fast away from that man but frequently looking back to see if the man was still following her. Around a corner she ran for it waving at the taxis passing by to stop for her but with no luck. She crossed the main road nearly getting hit by a fast-moving van leaving the driver fuming with rage. The woman ran as fast as she can, creating a gap between her and the stalker. She entered an office building and started talking to the security officer at the reception. Moments later the security officer left the building and stood outside on the pavement. A man as described by the woman was approaching. As soon as the security guard had seen the man, he pulled out his gun and aimed at the man. The man kept walking forward and as he was near the security guard the man flipped in the air three times landing first to his left position, then the right and the left again before drawing out a gun himself. The woman walked slowly toward the building's front glass windows to see what was going on before she screamed and ran toward the back of the office building. A gunshot sound made her stop for a second looking back to see what was going on. A huge fire door opened at the back of the office building and the woman ran as fast as she can to the other side of the city. Soon after she found herself among other shoppers frightened and scared. She looked everywhere scanning the entire area before disappearing among the people. Minutes later she suddenly stopped and dropped down all the designer bags she was carrying. She screamed, scared, and frightened. A man was standing in front of her looking at her with piercing eyes. For a few seconds, she had frozen up before running for her

life. The man instantly pulled a gun and shot at her
narrowly missing her as she fell to the ground. The
woman got up quickly and crossed the busy road
leaving the drivers blasting the car horns
continuously. She sped and safely crossed the busy
road and ran on the pavement bumping into the
pedestrians. The man ran after her and when he
reached the pavement, he looked at his watch and
aimed at the woman. He quickly fired a shot
missing her for the second time as the woman
suddenly disappeared around the corner. He ran
after her and as soon as she was in his view, he fired
another shot this time hitting the wrong person
leaving everyone taking cover. He chased after her
this time as fast as he can, determined to get her.
The woman looked back before looking to the other
side. The man placed his gun at his back and chased
after the woman. The woman quickly crossed the
road looking back to see if the man was following.
The man ran for a while and stopped as he heard a
beeping sound. He looked at his watch and looked
at the woman. The woman for a second or two felt
relieved to see that the chaser had given up. She
looked at the man and saw that he had stopped on
the pavement. She looked around and saw a car
coming her way very fast. She instantly stopped as
the car passed nearly knocking her down. As soon
as the car had passed, she looked back to see if the
man was still following her, but he was not. She
paced forward crossing the busy road. She looked
left and then right and proceeded. The road was
clear and was about to cross the last lane of a three-
lane road when the screeching of tires suddenly

caught everyone's attention. The man looked in the direction the van was coming from. The woman stopped for a second or two after hearing the screeching sound then proceeded and then stopped again a few feet away from the edge of the road. By this time a lot of people had gathered. The man and the onlookers looked at the coming van and instantly at the woman who seemed to have stopped in the middle of the last lane. "Run! Cross the road! Why have you stopped?" Shouted one of the onlookers fearing for the worst.

"Run! Cross the road!" shouted the onlookers but for some strange reasons, the woman appeared to have frozen in the middle of the last lane. She stood still not moving but facing the oncoming van. The man looked at his watch and smiled. All this happened in a few minutes, but it seemed like it took a long time. In slow motion, the woman only reacted at the last minute as she heard the van coming her way at full speed. All along she had been frozen still in the last lane. The onlookers covered their mouths in fear of what was going to happen. Some shouted and some even tried to run to her rescue, but it was too late. The van as if in slow motion plunged into the woman at full speed sending her flying into the air before she slumped back to earth and hitting the ground so hard that the onlookers heard a huge thump sound as she landed. Soon afterward blood ran out from her mouth and head as she lay on the road with her eyes wide open. The van screeched its tires before coming to a halt yard away. The man who was chasing the woman ran toward the van, opened the side door, and jumped in. Soon afterward the van screeched its tires before disappearing leaving the woman lying in the road blood flowing out of her body. A crowd started gathering around her and a few feet away cars stopped and parked meters away from the position the woman lay dead. The sound of sirens startled a few as the sound became more audible. Joseph one of the onlookers ran toward the woman as she lay dead on the road and knelt next to her checking her pulse.

"Why didn't she run and crossed the road?" He looked at everyone standing near the dead woman, but no one knew why, and no one could answer his question. Joe after playing the video stopped the video and walked toward the window.

"Power Viktor. Power. Power to control the universe. Power to decide who dies and when they die." Viktor looked upset and very angrily. He got up shaking with anger, fear, and confusion.

"You bastard! What makes you think that I want anything to do with such cold murder. I am a businessman. I worked hard for everything I have. I have morals. I will never be such a low-life. Damn, that could have been my daughter. Damn! I don't want anything to do with this. No. Get out of my office." Joe looked at Anita who in turn stood up and picked up the laptop before the two-started walking toward the door. Anita walked out of the office first and Joe was about to leave the office when Viktor coughed.

"Did you say something?" Joe peeped in. "No! OK, one more thing. What happened? Why didn't she cross the road? Why did she stop in the middle of the road especially when the van was coming toward her? She was looking at the van why didn't she jump out of the way?" Joe smiled and signaled to Anita to come back in. The couple entered the office. Anita looked sad and worried and a bit frightened, but Joe had a shining bright face like that of a young student about to open Pandora's box. "Power Viktor! Power. This is not for the faint-hearted. This is a power no other living man has witnessed. The power to control the entire world. Power to inherit the world's trillions and make them yours without anyone challenging you." Viktor looked frightened but interested to some extent. "$10 billion now."

"Still you didn't answer my question."
"Incapacitated! Imagine incapacitating all your enemies and these crooks stealing your customers. The possibilities are endless. Viktor the world is yours."

"$10 billion now."

"I don't want any innocent blood on my hands."

"Then you are not ready Viktor. Ask yourself why no one has ever managed to acquire such a fortune? To do that, you must be as cold-blooded as can be. I am giving you the opportunity to show the world power. Real power. Power to control everyone." Viktor looked scared. This was a dangerous road. This was against everything he had stood for. His business was in trouble. "Take it or leave it. I offer you this opportunity once. $10 billion now or you want me to demonstrate further." "What do you mean? Kill more innocent people?"

"Do you think you can ask people for their money nicely and they can just give you? Viktor don't waste my time. $10 billion or I will offer this to someone else." There was a moment of silence as Viktor hesitantly considered the offer.

"How can I get my money back?" Joe folded the sleeves of his shirt after removing his suit jacket. He looked at his watch and looked at Anita. Anita walked toward him and handed the laptop. Joe breathed heavily and requested Viktor to sit down. Anita took out a small box and placed it on the table. The box rebooted and after a while started flashing first red lights followed by the green lights.

"Come on! Come on!" said Joe looking at the laptop. He looked at his watch again. A beep sound sends Viktor and Anita panicking and a message was displayed on the screen.

"Synchronization in progress please wait." Ten minutes passed by and Joe was still playing with his laptop and the small box on the table.

"Are you sure this will work?" asked Viktor with some sense of doubt. Joe did not reply but sighed instead before looking at his watch again.

"Damn! I can't get any access."

"Maybe we keep on trying," added Anita with $10 billion in her mind. Another 20 minutes still there was nothing. Joe was having difficulties infiltrating the city system, but he looked very determined in getting this done. He had never failed, or should I say he never gave up and, in some cases, he had achieved what he wanted after he had considered giving up. Viktor at this time looked anxious. Morally this was something he would never do, but he was heading for disaster. He was losing money fast. His lifestyle was an extravagance and losing all that would be something unbearable to him. This was his only option all the five coastal companies were now losing money daily. Joe looked poised to make it, determined and focused. Failed attempts after failed attempts. Another twenty minutes went by this time Viktor had slumped back in his sofa. Anita was anxious too that she kept rubbing Joe's back. Surely $10 billion dollars was serious money even though they had just met Joe seemed to Anita like that kind of guy who would not let her down. Whatever it takes even if it means tiring her hand out Anita was determined to witness this too. It was Viktor who tried to ease the anxiety and impatience.

"You didn't explain why the woman did not move out of the road. This kind of doing my head-in."

"What?" Shouted Joe briefly looking at Viktor."

Anita rephrased the question.

"Oh. That woman. Yes. Because she couldn't."

"Do you mean you instantly froze her in front of oncoming traffic?"

"Perfect murder. Your hands clean and you have eyewitnesses. Problem solved."

"Still that does not explain why she did not scream or panic. Surely that is not human behavior."

"Viktor to be a Trillionaire you have to do what no other man has done. I have worked hard over these years since my father disappeared." The conversation carried on until a beep sound came from the small box followed by an automated voice.

"Entity acquired. Initializing and loading parameters. Please wait..." Everyone looked at each other with Viktor quickly sitting up straight on the edge of the sofa. Joe smiled and rubbed his hands before typing on the laptop quickly followed by beeping sounds. It was now almost fifty-seven minutes since they rebooted the small box. Joe quickly removed his wristwatch and placed it on the table next to the small box. He quickly typed some logarithms and functions and each time pausing before looking at the screen. A thorough list of functions and algorithms appeared and disappeared on the screen.

"I want to receive accounts of all your five coastal companies. Quickly." Viktor got up and took out his phone and scrolled quickly before putting it on the table in front of Joe.

"Will it not be traced back to me?"

"Don't worry about that, you are safe." Joe typed on the keyboard as fast as he can. He looked worried and anxious as well. Sweat droplets could be seen developing on his forehead that he kept loosening his tie. A beeping sound startled Joe causing him to stop for a while. This came from the small box followed by another beep from his watch. He looked at his watch. Fifty-nine minutes had passed since launching the small box.

"Come on. Come on!" shouted Joe as he looked at the small box. An automated voice interrupted him.

"Counting down. 60 seconds before shutdown." Joe looked at Viktor and briefly at Anita before opening his eyes wide and instantly looked back at the laptop screen. He typed as fast as he can quickly looking at the small box showing a countdown.

"45 seconds."

"30 seconds."

Everyone was silent, only the noise made by the laptop keyboard could be heard followed by Joe's heavy breathing. Anita and Viktor threw each other a quick glance.

"15 seconds to go."

"10 seconds."

"5 seconds,"

Quickly Joe pressed the enter button on the laptop and quickly another button on the small box. For a second the displayed time froze at 3 seconds.

"Come on!" shouted Joe clenching his fists before the small box started shutting down giving off the last beep.

"What happened?"

"What happened Joe," asked Viktor and Anita simultaneously.

"Damn!" Shouted Joe quickly looking at the laptop. He looked at Viktor with piercing eyes.

"I don't think it has gone through. I don't think I made it" He quickly typed on the laptop keyboard before he paused. Viktor and Anita leaned forward-looking at the laptop. It was now nearly one hour two minutes since the initialization of the small box. Joe stood up and walked toward the window. He was sweating. He stood at the window cooling down and cursing and rubbing his neck. The other two gazed at the laptop patiently. A beeping sound soon was released from the laptop. Quickly Joe ran to the table and sat in front of the laptop and typed something. He waited, and everyone threw each other a quick glance. Another deep sound and Joe stood up and shouted.

"Yes. $1 billion dollars."

"What?" shouted Viktor looking at Joe and then the laptop screen.

"Yes. $1 billion dollars." Anita got up and smiled. He dragged Joe to one side.

"If you can do this by yourself why you need him for?"

"It's not that easy. I need someone with billions already to carry a withdrawal- and-refill. That way no one can raise suspicion. It will look like just moving money between accounts."

"I don't want any problems or any silly tricks. Okay? Maybe buy $10 billion with $1 billion. Yes? I am not stupid you know." "It's not like that Viktor. I will carry out what I call a withdrawal-and-refill. To them, it will look like you are moving money between accounts. You make the perfect candidate."

"So, are you telling me that this money is in my

account now?" Asked Viktor a bit suspicious.

"No."

"No! What do you mean no? Where is this money right now? You said you have transferred?"

"It's not that simple. It is floating somewhere. In ghost accounts then after some time, it will reflect in your accounts. I will need a list of all your major customers and suppliers."

"How long will this take?"

"Not sure really never tried it on enormous amounts but normally between 2 hours to 30 days."

"30 days?"

"30 days yes. That way it won't be traced easily, and no one will notice quickly." "Honestly I don't think this will work. You were talking about trillions look how long it took you and how long it will take. No, I think I don't want anything to do with this."

"Viktor don't be short-sighted. This will work trust me. Now transfer out $1 billion to this account from one of your accounts. That will be replaced by the one we just got." Viktor looked at Anita and Joe before sitting down.

"If you play games with me, I will hunt you down and kill you myself." Joe smiled but Anita looked at

Joe with a face that seemed to ask Joe what the fuck was going on. Viktor transferred $1 billion and Joe and Anita left the big office building in the city center into Joe's Lamborghini and vanished. A red BMW sports car cruised on the motorway heading to the suburbs on the outskirt of the city center. In the car was David and Vicky. Vicky looked outside the window and saw buildings running backward as they drove forward. Vicky remembered what had happened to her in the office. A sudden strong feeling of fear crippled her. She felt a sudden rush of mixed emotions that left her undies wet. This was the most crippling fear-feelings she had ever experienced.

"Are you okay darling?"

David briefly looked at Vicky as he drove her back home.

"Everything is going to be alright."

Vicky did not say anything she just looked at him and soon after looked outside. She instantly had a scary flashback that elevated her heartbeat. She remembered seeing a message on the screen just before the computer switched off. Who was behind this? Surely this was more than a coincidence. What had gone into her causing that extreme intense orgasm? Surely someone or something was behind this. She was so sure that this was more than natural. What had happened to her? Why she couldn't see? What temporarily blinded her? What if this happened again? Fear crippled her and instinctively she grabbed David's arm.

"What's wrong are you sure you are okay. Don't worry we will soon be home."

The car arrived home and David and Vicky entered their mansion. Vicky looked lost, disoriented at times, and very scared even as she tried to hide it. "

"I want to take a shower come up upstairs with me?"

"Yeah sure."

The couple went upstairs, and Vicky took a long bath as they talked together.

"I don't know what is going on but today something bad happened."

"Darling you keep on saying that something bad happened but the way I saw you in that office, it doesn't seem like you were having a bad time. The more you say that the more I think you are trying to cover up something. What really are you saying?" Vicky sighed and closed her eyes covering them with both her hands.

"I think someone hacked the system through my account and...." David came toward the bathtub and sat on the edge rubbing Vicky's head.

"Why would someone hack your system and what can they possibly do? I understand your security system is robust."

"I thought so myself but what happened left me doubting the robustness."

"Are you saying that someone could steal money from the bank through the system?"

"Never done before that way as far as I know I mean from external sources. Mainly it's an inside job but what I witnessed today up to now I am still speechless."

"What makes you think that someone might have hacked your system?" Vicky sighed heavily and looked down for a while.

"A few seconds before you opened the office door a message appeared on the screen." Vicky looked at David and quickly in the foamy water between her legs.

"Yes. What happened?"

"A message appeared on the screen just seconds before system shutdown." Vicky looked at David for a while.

"A message? What did it say? I thought it was normal just before the lunch break."

"I think someone was making transactions through my account." David stood up and walked toward the mirror in the bathroom. He looked at himself for a while before turning to Vicky.

"Are you sure about that?"

"A message appeared on the screen. I am sure I have seen that message before but only after completing a money transfer." "Darling your computer might have frozen up just after your last transaction and then unfreeze minutes later that could explain the sudden shutdown." David sat down next to her on the edge of the tub.

"I did not make any transactions today." "What? I thought you said that you do that every day before lunch."

"Yes, but today..."

"Yes, I am listening."

"I was really horny. Thinking about you." "So, you couldn't wait for me? You would rather give yourself one. Oh, I feel hurt." "Listen to me. This is not a joke. When you came into the office, the displayed message read $1 billion transferred."

"Definitely an error who would transfer a $ billion in such a brief time without getting caught or crashing the system for that matter? I understand you will need authorization to transfer such kind of money. That means at least two security gates. Impossible."

"That's what I am thinking but I think whoever is doing this has more power and is more devious."

"What do you mean?" David stood up and looked at Vicky with the corner of his eyes. Vicky spread her legs wide open and looked at David who looked not amused before casting an unblinking wrathful face.

CHAPTER THREE

Outside a big mansion, a Lamborghini was parked within the boundaries of the high-security fence. Inside the bedroom, a woman was lying on the bed half-naked. The woman was sleeping on top of the bed covers with part of her legs hanging as she slept diagonally. She lay peaceful wearing white knickers and bra-less but sleeping on her stomach. For a moment she opened her eyes and turned around before going back to sleep. Upstairs Joe was busy on his computer entering formulas and algorithms. He cursed and got up before he pushed his hair backward. He picked up a remote control and pressed some buttons and instantly a song by Elinadeivid Let's plan our future Remix started playing. Joe got up and grabbed a bottle from the small refrigerator. He looked at the screen on the wall. It appeared as if a lot of rockets were being fired into the sky one after the other and as one landed another one rose into the sky and suddenly an error message would appear on the screen. Joe would start the program again. That went on for some time until Joe cursed and went down to the bedroom. Anita lay on the bed before she woke up and spoke to Joe.

"Why waking up so early? Come back to bed." Joe sighed and stood in the middle of the bedroom thinking of what to do.

"What seems to be the problem?"

"The program I am working on keeps on crashing."

"Yeah so keep on trying." Joe looked disappointed and scared. Anita raised her head before turning around and then sitting on the bed looking at Joe.

"Viktor."

"You tried the program and transferred some money, didn't you?"

"Yes, that was on a small scale. To get larger amounts requires a lot of time and an advanced program and the one I had envisaged keeps on crashing." Anita looked worried and scared too.

"Maybe let's not play games with him. Just tell him we cannot and let's just take the $1 billion and forget about all this." Joe sat down on the bed and looked on the bed before looking at Anita.

"We are already into this. I can't give up now. There is something we can do. I know somehow this is possible." After a while, Joe looked at Anita and suddenly realized how beautiful and sexy she was. She was half-naked, and her perfect boobs pointed at him. He looked further down and saw Anita's pubic hair piercing through her knickers. Joe laid down on the bed on top of Anita and the couple started kissing. Soon after Anita's legs were raised upward, and the two enjoyed making love. Later Anita got up naked and walked to the bathroom leaving Joe lying on the bed. Anita shouted something at the same time opening the water tape.

"Say that again?"

"I said what is the worst-case scenario?" Joe sat on the bed and shouted back.

"Viktor can kill us himself but..."

"But what?" asked Anita.

"We have a good chance of making this happen. I have to think of something either a fast program or find a way of getting more time." Joe got up and took his robe and went upstairs. Minutes later Anita followed wearing nothing. Joe looked at her figure. She was perfect. Tall well shaped with a beautiful face and a sexy smile. Her long legs made Joe drool that he felt like humping her all day long but there were more pressing issues to think about all that. Anita knew Joe was scared and worried. Viktor was no angel. He was an actor. A man who can become anything to get what he wanted. Deep down all the talking about morals and ethics was just one of his acting roles. People who knew him well knew that he was a ruthless monster behind closed doors. Joe, on the other hand, saw $10billion dollars as serious money for him to worry about insignificant fears. He saw this as a challenge.

"Well, what are you trying to do with your program?" Questioned Anita strolling nude like a model.

"Well, I need a fast program that can allow me to make a lot of transactions at the same time without crashing the system. The program I have will automatically crash the system before we can get any money out. Mind you we have a few minutes to do this." Joe looked at the screen on the laptop before getting up and looking at the big screen on the wall showing the same image. The couple looked at the screen before Anita opened Joe's robe getting inside his robe and hugged him. The couple worked for some time together with Joe creating algorithms and functions but every time the system crashed and immediately started shutting down the process. Every time they rebooted the computer and repeated the process again. Anita sat on Joe's lap naked and somehow Joe stopped what he was doing and caressed her for a while. Anita took Joe's hand and dragged him out of his seat and out of the room down to the bedroom. This time they stood next to the bed and Anita knelt and kissed Joe who appeared to be a little shorter than her. Each time Joe would lift his heels and kissed her before lowering his legs again. After a while, Anita was really turned on and passionately hugged Joe as the two made love. The couple made passionate love but soon afterward Joe had climaxed already leaving Anita gagging for more. Anita placed her hand on Joe's private parts and started playing with him before the two hooked in each other's arms again. Soon after both climaxed at the same time and lay on the bed for a while. Minutes later Anita woke up and walked to the bathroom.

"Flamingo, water, fish, talk, model, sexy, walking, flying big bird, kneels."

"What?" shouted Anita from the bathroom. "Word search. Brainstorming." Joe got up butt naked and ran upstairs to the study room. He quickly sat on his computer desk and typed something onto the laptop keyboard. After a while, he stopped and looked at the big screen on the wall. Rockets flew up one after the other before plunging down. Quickly Joe looked at his watch.

"Come on!"

Soon afterward the error message appeared on the screen.

"Damn!" Shouted Joe the moment Anita entered the study room.

"It crashed again."

"Crashed."

"The projections are haphazard that the computer is detecting the movements and considering these as unusual and therefore triggering a safety mechanism causing the system to crash and automatically causing the shutdown."

"These people are clever is that a security feature?"

"Yes, babes. But we must find a way around it. We need a way of making a lot of transactions within a brief period without crashing the system."

"Fucking, climax, fast, multiple orgasms, simultaneously," shouted Anita.

"You want to fuck again?"

"No. Word search. Brainstorming. Can I?" asked Anita pointing at the seat where Joe was seated. Anita minimized the program and looked for the Internet icon.

"I have your answer lover boy. Look at this," Anita opened a page showing flamingo's feeding.

"You said flamingos, right?"

"Yes. But..."

"Okay watch this. I think this is what you really want," Joe looked in anticipation wondering what that could be. A video started playing, and the two threw each other a quick glance. Joe looked with such a face that was asking what was that? "Wait for it. It's coming right now." Instantly a bird flew past a river before stopping in midair and instantly shoot down that fast into the water like a bullet. Anita looked at Joe's face before pointing at the screen.

"Now this is your answer. Look!" Joe looked astonished as the video showed the water turning red in a flash and something jumping out and back again into the water at lightning speed. Joe hugged Anita and kissed her.

"Get up quickly let me see," Anita smiled. "Sure partner."

"Oh yes partner 50: 50 yeah. I hope this works. This is the best of what I am trying to achieve."

"My dad used to say the best designs are from nature. When I saw your rockets falling quickly, I knew what you were looking for."

"That's really strange because it looks random and disorganized. The problem is that this might still cause the system to crash," he smiled.

"Any random chaotic transactions might activate the alarm. I must find a-way. Somehow this is the

answer. I must study this video. Thanks, sweetie."
Anita stretched her hand.

"Thank me downstairs."

"Right now?"

"Yes, Joe. I can tell you another secret." "Really?"
The couple went downstairs. "Listen. Don't think
about yourself only. I am your partner whatever you
do think about me as well. Imagine we are on the C
saw. You cannot go up without me on the other end.
I cannot go up without you on the other end. When I
go up you must be down and when you go up, I
must be down. I lift you and you lift me. It's the
same as making love. I know you are young and
inexperienced."

"Please, inexperienced me."

"Okay maybe you are experienced, but I am just
saying with the others namely my ex-boyfriends I
have multiple orgasms just because they know what
they are doing. They were there to make me orgasm
as well whereas you like your crashing program you
only think about yourself. You hurry everything. I
am just saying read the signs. I am like a book.
Look at all the commas, punctuation marks, the full
stops, and the paragraphs. Listen to the rhythm.
Look at my face's blood vessel patterns. When you
are experienced all this will be on your fingertips
and you will cook me perfectly and give me
multiple orgasms as well. I swear when you can do

that you will be able to run your program without it crashing." Joe looked astonished.

"It's not easy giving a woman the best time of her life. It comes with experience and as far as I can tell and from your crashing program you are an amateur in that department. So, what are you waiting for?" Joe leaned forward and kissed Anita.

"Kiss. Contact," whispered Anita. Joe quickly rubbed Anita's nipples.

"Friction. Stimulation," added Anita dragging Joe to the bed. Joe quickly placed his hand on Anita's groin.

"No Joe. Don't jump there. Make me horny first when I am ready you will know it." The kissing and smooching went on for some time until Joe could feel the rhythms and after observing Anita's face, he noticed blood vessels being filled with blood and by this time Anita was very wet he knew it was time. After a while, he could feel Anita's rhythm and contractions. Instinctively he intensified fastening his grips as well.

"I'm coming. Don't stop."

The moment he heard that he felt like letting go but only to hear Anita shout something else. "Don't move. Don't move." "Instantly he stopped and felt Anita rubbing herself very hard on him. The pleasure moans gradually increasing with every contraction. A fervid cry and a rush of blood to her cheeks and nipples set the roller coaster. He knew this was it. He intensified everything until the couple climaxed at the same time. Joe was about to slump down on the bed when Anita put her hands on his waist.

"Don't move. Hold still." Joe looked surprised to find out how those phrases quickly got him back on his feet again. This time Anita's rhythms had become so pronounced and fast and the blushing so intense. Fast and intense she wriggled her waist against his body before she climaxed again this time shivering with passion as having some tremors of some kind. Followed by another phase with intense contractions. This aroused Joe so much that the two got tangled again. For some reason, to Joe it was like the C saw again so synchronized and happening simultaneously. Joe visualized as if he was releasing some static electric currents that were making Anita shiver with passion letting out a soft cry. Soon after the speed increased so as Anita's cries and blushing as well.

"I got it. Every projection should be linked and there must be a signal or communication of some sort between every projectile."

"Don't talk. Faster. I'm coming."

Later that evening Joe was so sure he can do this. Anita had pointed him in the right direction. He watched the video again. The small greedy fish were the piranhas. Joe discovered that they worked in pairs. Like Anita had said they all communicated somehow. He realized that the fish pairs communicated using static electric currents. After a thorough observation, he noticed that a static electric current was exchanged between the fish. This made the fish jump out of the water and as soon as the fish gets back into the water as soon as the fish made contact with water a static electricity charge is released and passed to the other pair causing it to leap up and out of the water. The whole thing was systematized and organized rather than being haphazard and chaotic as he had thought. The fish attacked the bird so swift and organized although it looked random and disorganized Joe discovered that everything was organized and systematized. This was what was missing with his projections. There was a need for the catalyst. Weeks that followed Joe had sleepless nights programming the perfect model. The weeks that followed saw him either on his desk or making love to Anita so passionately and intense than he had done before. Trial after trial still the problem somehow crashed in the end because of a lake of time. But there was a big chance this time it would work. A tall beautiful woman walked into the city center before she suddenly stopped and closed her eyes. In a split second she pulled out a 44.44 Magnum revolver from her purse and instantly froze for a few seconds. Eyes closed, she turned 45' and fired a shot a few seconds later she turned another 45' and fired another shot and within a fraction of a second she had fired four shots before she opened her eyes. Suddenly a man appeared in front of her and in a split second he had disappeared. The woman looked at her revolver and smiled and instantly a loud cry of pain is heard 45 degrees of her position. As she turned to watch a man who had appeared a fraction of a second before lay in a pool of blood. The woman walked toward him and knelt close to him and picked up his gun and looked at him.

"Poor thing. Too slow. I got you. Damn, I am good."

She stood up and looked around and walked away from the scene and the moment she looked back she saw a crowd approaching surrounding the man as she disappeared around the corner. Moments later an SUV emerged from the upper floor car park and revved before speeding on the highway.

"Hey, Californika. Just to let you know that the show starts at 3 pm. I guess you already ready. No fucks up this time. See you there." After listening to the message Californika looked in the side mirror before speeding off. Mark was a very strict man these two have known each other since they were in high school. Mark had seen a raw talent in Californika. She was hot. I mean Damn hot for her age. A very attractive blond, tall, hot lady, with sexy blue shining eyes and a smile to match. She was very tall and sexy with a booty that fits perfectly in line with her body proportion. Mark had seen real potential and over the years he had cultivated and pampered that raw talent hoping that one-day Cali would make him rich. She had appeared on TV commercials, in magazines, at fashion shows you name it. The girl was such an angel that everyone liked her. There was something about her. She was different from all the other girls. Everywhere she goes people would instantly fall in love with her. Mark and Cali had been together for quite some time now and those who saw them thought that they were a perfect couple mainly because of the chemistry between them but, they were just friends. Mark was small and weak but very intelligent. A man who knew what he really wanted from anyone. He was persistent that in the end he always got what he wanted. At first, Cali had resisted his charms. Honestly Mark was way out of Cali's ideal man. She wanted a strong man, physically, and mentally. A man so ruthless and cold that no one would appreciate him. Her friends always thought that she was weird somehow, but she didn't give a fuck. A few years down the road she had met Viktor. A cold-blooded killer behind closed doors and an angel in the public arena. Viktor was too faced. Those who really knew him knew he was the best actor they had met. They knew if he was in Hollywood Viktor would win an Oscar. He was that good at role play that those who didn't know much about him would be strayed away by his charms and so-called kindness. When Californika first met Viktor, she sensed his dark side although it took a lot more convincing before Viktor admitted, she was so sure she had found a partner. When Mark discovered that Californika was seeing Viktor he couldn't understand it. Viktor had always loved the smallest, needy, clingy women around. Women who would show him emotions and cry all the time on his shoulder. Women who always showed him affection. Women who were always by his side. Californika didn't give a damn about man. Most of her friends especially Mark had thought that she was neutral with no sexual appetite at all. Mark recalled all those nights they had spent together without any chemistry despite his advances and all the romantic gestures. She was hot with big round pointing tits and the booty any man would want to cling onto but somehow, she behaved like she had a lot of testosterone than progesterone. Mark recalled one night when she came back home excited and full of life. She kicked the doors around and jumped on the couch. Mark couldn't believe it. She was like a little girl in love. She grabbed the sofa cushion and covered herself wearing only some hot white knickers. This was the first time in years Mark had seen her partly naked. All these years she had acted like a tomboy wearing big t-shirts and baggy track bottoms. That night she had met the monster the man who would convert her. The man she really loved. The man she craved for. She had explicitly spilled the beans. I mean everything that had happened between the two. Mark recalled watching her bending down and pulling down her saucy white knickers halfway down only to show him the marks on her buttocks, marks which were left by Viktor. Mark couldn't believe it. Viktor had stolen the innocence of this woman. She had lost her innocence, or should I say, her security and morals as well turning her into a horny confused lady. He remembered one of his friends explaining that what Viktor only did was to awaken Cali's dormant feelings and blaming him would not be fair. They had had wild sex. He had used a sharp razor blade to cut very small incisions on her buttocks while they did it somehow, he knew what she really wanted. The candle droplets didn't do the magic. To Mark, this was beyond his scope. He had never imagined doing something like that. He recalled listening when she talked. He could still see her face radiant and fervidly struck with passion. The excitement on her face. The smile, the laughs, the giggling. He very much remembered the mixed feelings that went through him as he listened. The feelings, of rage, love, jealous and the feelings of happiness for her. For the first time he saw a different lady. She spoke to him in detail about everything as if she was talking to her girlfriend. Only if she knew he was about to burst with lust and cravings for her but honestly, she just wanted a listening ear so that she can relive the encounter. Viktor had turned her inside out. Ever since Mark, unlike other men, had worked hard securing lucrative contracts for her. Viktor was a very rich man and Mark knew he was out of his league and would not stand any chance. The fear of losing her gave him sleepless nights. California was such an angel. A rare charm. One of a kind. Surely, she was worth competing for. The modeling deal gave him a great advantage over Viktor. Californika wanted to be independent and self-reliant. Mark knew Viktor was the kind of man who would throw money around in exchange for total control something Californika disliked. She wanted to do her stuff and if sex with Viktor then it was according to her terms and will. Something Viktor disliked. Since she met Viktor she had canceled numerous appointments and never attended some very important modeling shows leaving Mark fuming. Mark recalled just a few weeks ago when she phoned an hour late telling him that Viktor had whisked her away on his private jet. That same night she had returned home very late at night with a gun in her purse. The following weeks she had started going out without coming back. Viktor was throwing money at her that in the end she saw no reason to spend hours on the catwalk. Slowly Mark started seeing a different lady in her. The smiling had vanished, and she had become very moody. He remembered her pointing a gun at him one day he opened her bedroom door. She was cautious about everything after that. She started spending money on guns instead of sexy knickers as she used to. He recalled one day her coming back home with blood-stained clothes. Mark checked his watch and looked around. The crowd had gathered and there was no sign of her.

"Where is she?"

"No idea. She should be here half an hour ago. Hopefully, she will make it before her turn."

"Don't count on it ten minutes is a small-time mate. The changing and the makeup. No way to forget it. I will shield in my spare instead with your blessings of course." "Give me time. She will be here."

"You know you said that the last time." "Come on. I have a lot going on. I said she will be here. OK?"

"OK if you say so."

Mark took out his cell phone and dialed again.

"Where are you?"

"In the dressing room. Don't worry I am ready." Mark clapped his hands very excited and headed toward the dressing rooms walking very fast. He knocked on the door and opened the door to find Californika in her undies.

"Nothing to be ashamed of my dear. It's a lingerie night. This is the big bucks."

"But I thought it's the summer dress night? Lingerie? Are you sure?"

"Do you have a problem with the lingerie theme?" Californika raised her eyebrows and opened her arms.

"Not really."

"So why you look frightened. You should be rejoicing. Isn't this what you have always wanted?"

"A lot of things have changed since then."

"What things. I see only an even perfect body. You have grown into a perfect angel. Everyone will love you. Just be yourself and everything will be perfect. Okay." Mark left the room soon after. The crowd cheered as lingerie models walked on the catwalk one after the other. Flashing clicks and lights blinded and deafened the models and everyone watching. Constantly they covered their eyes to avoid direct flashes. It was hilarious for everyone involved. People cheered and clapped their hands. Photographers edged forward lining the bottom of the catwalk taking pictures at different angles as the models paraded themselves. The judges sitting just along the catwalk typed something on the handheld tablets as the women paraded themselves in lingerie. Mark looked at his watch and looked at the hallway expecting Californika anytime soon. As soon as the other model disappeared. A tall very beautiful lady with curly hair in small sexy knickers and a matching bra appeared and stood for a while, unlike her mates. She posed and looked around. For a fraction of a second everyone looked and paused clapping hands, but the flashing intensified. Mark looked at Californika. "Don't be scared. Be yourself. I know you can do it," whispered Mark.

Californika looked around anticlockwise before she started strolling. Everyone went berserk cheering, and everyone stood up and clapped hands whilst others started whistling. The photographers went made and shot as many photos as they can.

Although this seemed like a stunning entrance to the catwalk Mark knew something was up. Californika had changed. Surely something was bothering her. She had been very scared of everything lately. She had appeared very unsettled on several occasions. Mark just prayed that this was not one of those nights. This is what he had wanted. One thing that calmed his nerves was the fact that the crowd loved her. She was unique, tall, and very beautiful. She was a very special lady. She made the other girls look second class. She was a hit with photographers as everything on her looked zoomed already, those lovely big tits and a cleavage that left many drooling. The whistling and clapping of hands as she strolled on the catwalk gave Mark goosebumps. He knew she would score high with most of the judges. Everyone smiled and loved her. Every time she stopped and posed putting her hands on her waist sends the crowd into a frenzy. She walked the catwalk once and then back again this time strolling sexy and a bit faster than the first time. She reached the end of the catwalk and made a U-turn. The cheers deafened everyone. The flashing intensified as this was her last catwalk in the lingerie category before someone else takes center stage. Mark clapped hands hard and cheered. California strolled the catwalk showing her assets until she was halfway and suddenly she stopped and ducked covering her eyes. Photographers leaned on the stage to take pictures. Everyone cheered except Mark. Mark quickly pushed forward near her. He looked around to see if someone was in the crowd who she might have feared. The first person to come to mind was Viktor. He thought that she might have been ashamed to be seen modeling by Viktor but after second thoughts this didn't make any sense. He jumped on the catwalk and this time Californika was on her knees with her eyes closed as if listening in deep concentration. She only opened her eyes when Mark touched her hand.

"What's wrong? What happened? Are you okay? You are now scaring everyone." Californika looked around in the crowd in an anticlockwise direction before getting up and strolling on the catwalk. No one seemed concerned. Everyone thought that this was a stance and instantly everyone loved it, especially the photographers who had taken several shots as she knelt there. Something that was not common. The crowd cheered as she stood at the doorway and posed for the final time before she disappeared. Mark ran outside and toward the dressing rooms. It took minutes longer before Mark heard the crowd cheering again for the next model. Breathing very hard, Mark opened Californika's dressing room without even knocking. She was in the bathroom pouring water on her face. "Are you okay? What happened out there? Is it Viktor?" Californika looked sad and worried. She took the big towel and covered her face dosing off the water on her face.

"It is Viktor, isn't it? But I thought he knew you do this?" Californika walked into the dressing room and looked at the big mirrors in front of her.

"You looked like you saw a ghost out there. Tell me what is going on?" Mark looked at her as she sat down in her lingerie.

"Are you going to tell me or what?"

"I don't know."

"What do you mean you don't know?"

"I felt something. OK?"

"Something. You looked like you fell into a trance of some kind on the catwalk." "Someone might have been there. I was scanning the area."

Mark looked shocked to hear that.

"Of-course there was everyone. Photographers, I mean everyone. Is that why you ducked is someone after you. Is it Viktor?"

"I thought I felt someone. Someone bad," Mark looked worried.

"If someone is after you do you duck, or you run away?"

"Listen. Like I said I reacted just an instinct. Don't spoil the night."

"But if something that bad is going on should I not know.? Is that why you spend your money on guns?"

"I am not that lady you used to know. A lot has changed."

"What has changed?"

"Mark. Can we talk about this some other time? Okay? How did I do?"

Mark's face changed from a worried face to a happy excited face.

"You nailed it. They loved you. No doubt I was surprised even after that incident they loved you even more. I can't wait to see tomorrow papers."

"Just hope no one took embarrassing photos of me flashing my..."

"Who cares it is the world of modeling you can expect anything."

"Me kneeling down flashing my..."

"What matters is that they loved you. You were great. It was excellent. Even the incident I think people thought you were trying to be different. The flashing and cheering. Out of this world. What an entrance. At one moment I thought nerves got you." Californika looked worried for a while.

"Oh. Nowadays I am not myself. I started feeling

things you know. It's like someone is there following me."

"Stay away from Viktor. He is dangerous enough." Californika stood up and leaned against the mirrors removing makeup from her face. "You should be mine. I mean you and I should be a couple you know. We go a long way. It tears me apart to hear you glorifying this monster. I heard some bad stories about him you know. I don't want to end up losing you, you know."

"What happened to no mixing business with pleasure?"

"We are making money. I can make you feel powerful too. You don't need Viktor to carry a gun or that you know. I loved you since I met you years ago."

"Please as if you can fuck me? You like to own me like I am your property. You can never be like Viktor."

"I can be the man you want. Give me this chance. We can make it together. Look we are now making real bucks."

"You don't understand I was never into this money thing. You still don't know what I want. Do you?"

"A powerful man. A rich man. A man who let you be yourself. Right." Californika turned and looked at Mark. Mark looked at her pubic region and at her pointing breasts as she removed her bra before looking up and looking straight into her eyes. Californika pressed herself against Mark and instinctively Mark leaned forward and kissed her lips holding her booty so tight that he felt blood running down his pants very fast. Californika pushed Mark to the chair and reached for her purse and took the revolver out. She licked the end of the barrel and pointed the gun at Mark and opened her big blue eyes. "You want to fuck me? Right? Do you know I am an assassin? A ruthless killer. You want this? Show me that you are a man Mark," Mark looked shocked.

"I thought it was for self-defense. What are you doing? Is that thing loaded?"

"You said you know what I want. Right? You want this?" Californika pointed her pubic area with the tip of the gun before pointing the gun at Mark and about to unfasten the belt of his trousers when Mark got up.

"Hey what are you doing? Is that thing loaded?"

Californika looked at Mark and started laughing.

"The look on your face. Damn you are scared. You make me laugh."

"So, are we fucking or what?"

"Viktor's unless..."

Said Californika licking Mark's cheek.

"Unless what?" asked Mark.

"Forget about it."

"No, come on tell me."

Californika pressed hard on Mark and whispered in his ears. It's a beautiful day in the nearby suburbs. A car approached and screeched its tires before coming to a halt in the middle of the road. A woman looked outside the window and caught a quick glimpse of the car. The driver looked back but remained in the car. Minutes passed by before another driver blasted the horn as his car approached. The driver looked at the woman still looking through the window before driving off. After a while, the woman disappeared from the window as she closed the curtains behind her. The car drove for a while before the driver made a U-turn screeching the car tires. He drove for a while and when he was where he had previously stopped he stopped the car. "Perfect Geo-locational position." An automated voice came from a small box on the dashboard. The man quickly got out of the car and looked around. He looked back into the car and pressed a button on the small box attached to the dashboard and at the same time a clicking sound is released from his wristwatch. He looked around and adjusted the watch before pulling out his gun. He walked a few steps ahead of the car and stopped in the middle of the road. He looked around and then at his watch and waited. As soon as the stopwatch had started ticking the man ran as fast as he can, circling the car radially stopping at every point every time he heard a click sound. He circled the car and was about to repeat the process when he heard a speeding car coming from the other end. He quickly got into his car and quickly drove off making a loud sound that the woman who was looking at him earlier on opened the corner of the curtain and looked only to see the car speeding away before another car passed at such a high speed that she did not see whether it was a man or a woman driving the car. The car that then stopped and parked some miles away and the man cursed and quickly took out a laptop from the back and onto the passenger seat and synchronized with the small box. A big circle appeared on the screen and soon after points were marked on the circled at angles of 30'. Instantly another circle is superimposed on top. The man looked at the red points which started flashing on the screen. A quick automatic calculation was carried out by the laptop and a time estimate was displayed.

"Damn! Not even close enough."

Cursed the man before looking around and driving off back to the point again. This time he parked nearby and looked around and when the road was clear and the neighbors not looking, he drove back to the position and soon after the small box flashed the green light. He got out and took a long breath and repeated what he did the first time. He looked at his wristwatch and started sprinting very fast circling the car. He quickly stopped as soon as he had heard a beep sound this time at every 45 degrees until he had completed the circle. He quickly stopped after the complete revolution and peeped inside his car. The calculations went on and the circles superimposed on top of each other. The first three points he was way out only the last point matched. He cursed again and repeated the entire process. Three times more he was still out. Another car interrupted everything. He drove off and reappeared after a while. The first round after reappearing was very close. Another trial and the first three points matched. Another trial saw a smile on his face. He opened the back door of his car and took out a silencer from the briefcase at the back and screwed it on. He looked around. Seconds later he initiated the small box and synchronized with his watch. A click sound saw him sprinting circling the car and as soon as a click went off from his watch he quickly knelt and fired a shot and instantly started running again circling the car at every 45 degrees. He shot eight times. Quickly once he had finished, he pressed a button on his watch and then the small box. A boy ran outside and picked up a newspaper that had just been dropped by a drone and ran back inside the house. A man was in the kitchen seated at the kitchen table having his breakfast.

"What's so special about today daddy?"

The man took the newspaper from the boy and opened it. He ate his sandwich and looked at the boy. The senator is coming to our neighborhood. Be a good boy okay. Stay in the fence don't go outside. Too many cars in the street today. Okay?"

"OK daddy but can I watch as he passes through?" The father looked at the paper for a while before replying.

"Yes, but keep the gate closed at all times." The man later left the house and waved goodbye to a woman whom he kissed standing at the door with a small boy. The big SUV left the family fence into the main road and the boy chased after it and stood at the gate before the car disappeared. The woman walked back into the house and looked outside the window for a while before going to the bathroom. The boy went inside the house and grabbed some sandwiches before heading outside. The woman started dozing off in the tub only to be woken up by a dog barking. Soon after it started to make sense as the noise got louder and louder. Neighbors walked outside and stood outside as the senator passed by with his entourage. Some people watched from the windows. Kristine quickly got out of the tub and put on a robe before shouting for her son. "Dennis! Dennis.!"

She ran outside to find her son stood at the gate.

"Come inside. Too many cars outside."

The boy struggled whilst holding onto the gate rails.

"But daddy said it's okay as long as I am inside the fence."

"Better view inside come now."

The woman and the boy struggled and finally, the boy was carried inside wriggling his legs.

"But I want to watch from outside. Daddy said it's okay. Mummy."

"I know listen to me let's watch from inside together. Okay."

"Oh, mummy. Let me watch from the gate." The dogs barked as the entourage passed by. The car in front edged forward with bodyguards scanning everywhere. The kids and some women lined up the fences as the entourage passed by. The vehicle in front with the bodyguards passed one of the houses and as the limousine carrying the senator followed, suddenly the car died, as the engine suddenly stopped. It took a few seconds before the car in front noticed that something was wrong as the limousine carrying the senator had stopped. "Ambush! Ambush!"

The bodyguards went out of the SUVs and shielded themselves behind these SUVs quickly glancing and scanning the area. One of the bodyguards noticed a curtain suddenly closing as someone peeped through the blinds and curtains and instinctively fired a couple of shots. The bodyguard in the SUV behind the limo heard a buzzing sound made by a shot coming from the direction he was facing as it passed him and instinctively he looked in that direction. Briefly, he saw what appeared to be a person standing behind the window and opened fire.

"Drive! Drive! Ambush! Drive Damn it. Drive," shouted the bodyguard at the back of the limousine but there was no answer he looked beside him after hearing the windows of the limousine shattering only to find the senator bleeding profusely.

"He has been shot, drive. Drive Ambush." "No electronics. The limo just died." "What?"

"Limo dead. Can't drive."

"Ambush. Ambush. I repeat send back up." The bodyguards ducked inside the limousine as the windows got shattered several times in seconds. The bodyguards in the SUVs in front and back returned fire. Far away a woman smartly dressed was in the office signing some documents when there was a quick knock at the door followed by the sudden opening of the door.

"Urgent phone call line 3."

"We have a problem. The senator entourage is under attack as we speak." "Attacked by who?"

"Not clear. I understand been ambushed." "Send back up straight away."

"Copy that."

Soon afterward the line went dead. The smartly dressed woman looked confused for a while not knowing what to do or think. Soon after she dialed a number and spoke on the phone. Minutes later she stood up and paced up and down next to the window briefly looking outside. A car suddenly appeared at the gate and the automatic gates slowly opened. It took a few minutes, but it seemed as if forever. The woman waited impatiently before a man dressed in uniform entered the office yard. He walked very fast and knocked on the office door.

"What's the update?"

"It doesn't look good too many deaths,"

"Is he dead? Who attacked him? Are they dead too?" The man looked sad as he looked downward.

"Been shot several times. Dead at the scene."

"Did they kill the shooters? How did this happen? Who else died?"

The man took a long breath. A car left the car park and straight onto the road. Inside was Marius in his late thirties. It had been a long day at work for him.

Finally, it was time to go home to his wife and kid. The car slowed down at the traffic light and Marius looked ahead before a woman and a boy on the pavement caught his attention. The boy was slightly older and taller than his boy. Looking at him made him realize that he hadn't been for his son. He recalled working even weekends both at work and at home. He knew somehow, he had neglected his family to some extent. Work had been demanding of late. The sound of the car horn and the shouting startled him and that had woken him up from daydreaming. It was only a few seconds or minutes and the lights had changed to green. Marius looked ahead and quickly drove away from the traffic lights and soon he was on the motorway heading home. As soon as he had left the motorway he drove for a while before entering the suburban area. Minutes later he started seeing a long queue of cars ahead of him. His car slowly joined the queue. He peeped out through the side window and saw something like a checkpoint ahead. A lot of flashing lights were seen ahead of him. His heartbeat raced for a while before suddenly calming down. He smiled. He remembered talking to his son that morning. Damn was the senator still in the neighborhood? He thought to himself. What was he up to? This was the newly appointed senator. He had been campaigning, visiting all the neighborhoods of late trying to get to know the people. Politics was a dirty game for Marius. He had done what he can to distance himself from all this especially when Kristine fell pregnant. After a while, the cars ahead of him came to a halt. He watched the drivers in front getting out of their cars. He looked next to him and took out his cell phone and jacket and got out as well. He followed the drivers ahead as they headed to the front of the queue. He looked ahead and saw blinding blue and orange flashing lights. Ahead seemed to be military personnel of some kind. The people stood behind a checkpoint barrier. The road into the main suburb had been cordoned off. He stopped, and a sense of fear gripped him. Surely something bad might have happened. He took out his phone and as he was about to dial his wife a car suddenly arrived from inside the suburb at high speed with flashing blue lights on top. Instantly the doors opened, and a man got out and straightened his suit and marched toward the checkpoint. The crowd that had gathered behind the check-point urged forward. Marius pushed the people trying to get as close as possible. "What is going on?"

"Why the road has been closed? We have our families in there."

"Let us in right now."

Shouted the crowd. The man in a suit stood in front of the crowd of drivers and other local people and raised his hands to shoulder level. A man in uniform walked toward the man in a suit and handed him a handheld louder speaker. "Listen very carefully. No one is allowed beyond this barrier until further notice." The crowd went berserk.

"What! We have our women and children in there.

We live here. This is our neighborhood. Why can't we enter? No. Let us pass right now."

The huge buzz and shouting suddenly stopped as the man address the crowd again.

"Everything is okay. Once we have finished what we are doing, you will all be allowed to enter. Bear with us soon the road will be open."

"Why no one is answering the phone." "Listen. Bear with us and soon you will have access."

"No. You Listen. Why our families are not answering our calls?"

The man looked at the other men in uniforms besides him.

"It's a security matter once the senator has left all phones will be fully operational." "What is going on? Are you hiding something from us?"

"Once we have finished. We will answer all your questions."

Hughes got really upset and pushed forward. "I never heard anything like this before. We have women and children there. My wife is there. My sons and daughter are in there. I have listened to you for the past hour now. I am going home to my family. Stop me if you can." Hughes climbed the checkpoint before getting his leg tangled for a few seconds. The men in uniform quickly pointed the gun at him.

"You want to shoot me?"

Shouted Hughes very upset. The man in a suit looked at the men with guns who in turn then pointed the guns down.

"Please bear with us. Stay back until we have cleared the area. Okay."

"You bastards. You want to shoot me? This is my family we are talking about."

"They have orders to shoot if you disobey my commands. In the meantime, everyone stays behind that checkpoint. Okay."

The man in a suit walked away from the crowd and into the car before he was instantly driven away back into the suburban area. A huge buzz suddenly followed as the crowd started discussing what they had just witnessed.

"All phone lines are dead. No reception at all. They must have switched off the nearest mast. Bastards. How can I tell if my family is okay?" shouted Brian.

"They can't keep us out for too long. Sooner or later they have to let us in."

"What if our families are in danger? We just wait

here?"

The men looked at each other before throwing a quick glance at the uniformed military personnel.

"They are not going to shoot. Trust me." "What if they opened fire on us?"

"Our families might be in danger."

"We can't just stand here."

"Brian is right. We have been here for some time now."

Soon after that, the military people threw each other a quick glance. They realized that the crowd was planning something. They inched forward and pointed the guns at the crowd.

"Don't even think about it. Step back."

"Or what? Shoot us," shouted Hughes. "Yes. I will shoot. Step back right now." "He's bluffing," shouted Enoch. The crowd started pushing forward shaking the checkpoint barrier. The crowd kept advancing and the other military person came out of the cars.

"Step back or we will shoot."

"Shoot us. This is our neighborhood. Shoot us for what?" shouted the mob.

"Step back!" The military personnel formed a line all aiming their guns at the crowd. One of them radioed someone.

"He is calling for backup. This is it or else never," shouted Hughes. The crowd suddenly pushed forward breaking the barrier on the second attempt.

"You can't stop us. You can't get away with this."

"Stop! Stop or I will shoot you."

Shouted the leader of the military personnel. They all stood their ground ready for action. Miles away a boot kicked one of the doors open and two men rushed into the house one after the other scanning the whole area. They headed upstairs once the two signaled the all-clear sign. On the steps, the men ducked and looked at each other as they had heard a noise coming from the room upstairs. One signaled to the other and pointed. Instantly one of them took off looking everywhere quickly and pointing a gun shifting from left to right all the time. As soon as he had reached the door, he knelt and first signaled to the other man who instantly followed his footsteps up the stairs. The other man arrived, and they both looked at each other. In front of them was a pool of blood coming from the room. They both stood beside the door on opposite sides. Immediately one kicked the door open before he ducked instantly.

"Help. Help."

Cried a woman on the floor clutching her side in a pool of blood. The men looked at each other for a while. One of the men knelt and instantly looked at the other. Instantly gunshots are heard from a distant, and the two men ducked for cover. The voice from the radio startled everyone especially the woman who lay in a pool of blood.

"We need back up as soon as possible."

The two men looked at each other before one of them took the radio from his shoulder and answered.

"We have a situation here. CV shot and bleeding to death."

"CV are you sure?"

"Sure."

"Any sign of armed militia?"

"CV only badly hurt need help as soon as possible."

"Have to get back to you on that one." "Help. Help. Please."

Said the woman in a soft voice as she lay on the floor.

"Help is on the way. Hang in there."

Said one of the military men. The other man looked very upset and got up and left the room before the other one followed him.

"Why did you say that?"

"She asked for help."

"But you know there is no help to come." "How do I know that?"

"Don't be a smart ass with me."

"I don't know what you are talking about." "If they were going to send help. He could have just asked ask to call the ambulance." The other man looked down.

"I understand the mast is down as well." The other man did not reply but just looked at his partner. A man in military uniform walked fast to one of the cars and entered inside.

"Get me the President right now."

Soon after the car screeched its tires and made a U-turn heading toward the road leading to the suburb entrance. Four other vehicles followed all flashing blue lights. As soon as the cars had arrived, the men jumped out all holding guns and marched toward their men in front of the crowd. The crowd stood there for a while shouting and requesting to speak to the man in charge. The back door of one of the cars opened and a man wearing a suit came out. He shoved what looked like a gun at his back trousers and walked toward the crowd.

"We want to see our families. Let us in right now." Shouted the crowd.

"What's going on. We need answers right now. We were waiting for more than an hour now. Tell us what's going on. let us in right now." Shouted Hughes. Hughes was a well-built man, very tall and often seen as the representative of the neighborhood even though he was not appointed by anyone. He would voice concern whenever the ordinary men would not. That night he had assumed the role of the leader of the crowd. Those who knew him knew that he was a loner. He had no family of his own. He was living with his mum. He had no kids. To him, this was an opportunity to represent every man with a wife and kids. Surely something more was going on than what they were being told. All men and women were afraid for their loved ones. The military men pointed guns at the crowd as the men approached closer to the crowd.

"You have been warned. Please listen very carefully," soon after the huge buzz died down.

"We want answers now. Let us see our families. Now," shouted Hughes. There was a moment of silence.

"OK. But we can't let everyone in at the same time. We will take one by one. What I need from all of you is your ID and name of your wife and all kids and address. Once you have provided this, then we can take you to your house. Okay." The men looked at each other surprised and some happy that some pushed forward taking IDs from their wallets.

"Okay follow one of these officers. Please. Okay."

The crowd rushed in a queue with their IDs in their hands. Marius stood there for a while pondering what all this was about. Surely something was not right. Why not just say the drive to your houses? Why give all that information for? Why they must take us there? Were their families in danger? A sudden feeling of fear hit Marius sending him shivering. He looked at everyone and saw Hughes in the queue as well. He remembered that technically Hughes had no one to fight for, unlike every other man. His mother had left and as far as he knew she was now in the residential homes somewhere far away. He stood there for a while and suddenly he started walking to his car. No one seemed to bother. He looked at his phone and still there was no reception. He opened his car and took out his gun and searched for a torch which he shoved in his jacket pocket. He looked around. Now it would not matter which way he goes in better alone than accompanied he thought to himself. Minutes later Marius was in the surrounding woods. It was getting dark. They had been there for nearly an hour and a half others even more than that.

Marius walked as fast as he can. He cursed as he realized that is what he should have done a long time ago. His heart started to beat very fast with every step as he advanced toward the suburb area. He remembered walking the dog with his son in these woods. He stopped for a while and looked at his cell phone. Still, there was no reception at all. A creepy sound in the woods made him duck. He drew out his gun and scanned the whole area. A few seconds later he was up again. He entered the suburb's wooden fence and could see some houses. Suddenly he heard a car engine and saw car lights approaching. He ducked in the woods and waited for the car to pass. The car drove past him but suddenly screeched its tires to a stop and reversed. Marius ducked scared and frightened. The car stopped near where he was hiding and turned onto the road in front of him. Marius got up and started walking toward his home but suddenly stopped and walked back and into the other street where the car had gone. He hid among the bushes and followed the car. After a few minutes of walking he saw the car stopped with all the doors opened and lights on. Marius came out in the open as he neared the parked car outside the house. He walked toward the car before he heard a woman screaming. He quickly ducked into the bushes as he heard the door of the housed being slammed shut. A man carrying a struggling woman came out of the house followed by the other military man holding the man. The woman struggled as she was carried into the car. The third military man came out carrying a young baby and gave the baby to the woman before

running in front of the car into the driver seat and
drove away. The car soon disappeared around the
corner. Marius remained ducked for a while before
he got up. He looked around and started running
toward his house. Suddenly as soon as he had
turned into the road leading to his house. He saw
cars parked outside one of the houses. On second
look he realized who lived at that address. It was
Wilfred. Suddenly a man came out running from the
yard of the house onto the streets. The two military
men followed onto the streets with guns raised. As
soon as the running man had turned into the yard of
another house on the left. Both the military men
stopped and instantly knelt with both their knees
touching the ground. They looked like they were
scanning the area and in a split of a second they
fired the shots. Immediately both got up but
instantly the other one ducked both knees on the
ground again but this time facing the direction in
which Marius was hiding. Marius looked around
him before ducking even further. A buzz sound near
his ear near crippled him with fear.

"Probably an animal."

"I will go and investigate."

"Let's retrieve the subject before someone sees
him." Shouted one of the men walking toward the
yard of the house where Wilfred had run onto. The
other man stood there for a while looking in the
direction where Marius was hiding. He started
walking in the direction where Marius was hiding.

"We don't have time. Check it later. Come."

The man stood there and looked for a while toward Marius before shoving his gun away. Marius' heartbeat was at its highest. He could hear his eardrums vibrating as well to the beat. For a second or two, fear had crippled him. He had never been this frightened before. Surely something bigger had happened. Soon after that, he heard that the footsteps toward him had stopped. He slowly raised his head and saw the man going away from him toward the other man. As soon as the man had disappeared into the yard of the house, he got up and ran as fast as he can away from the scene hiding among the bushes. When he was away from the house, he stopped and looked as he had heard voices. The men came out carrying a dead body he presumed. They were holding his hands and legs and his head looked slumped and lifeless. Fear crippled him and instantly he started running away. One of the men let go of the dead body sending it down with a thumb and instantly he was on his knees before he fired consecutive shots. The other man ducked as well landing on his knees and fired shots at an angle to the first man. Marius had turned the corner so fast without even knowing it. Seconds later he opened his eyes and blinked before seeing the green grass. He felt a cold feeling that instantly disappeared as a warm feeling of running warm water like soon covered his body. He smiled when he saw his son standing at the gate. Good boy. He thought out loud. He felt very excited and started running toward him dropping his jacket and work files. He tried very hard but somehow, he could not seem to arrive at where he was. A strange feeling paralyzed him as the boy started drifting away.

"Sean. Sean. Sean!"

The huge wooden doors flung wide open as a man wearing white gloves entered the building. Behind him was a man well dressed up in a suit with well-combed hair. The look on his face said it all. Something big had happened. This man would normally cast a quick smile every time he met one of his personnel, but this day was not like any other. They walked across the hallway until they have reached another huge door with golden door handles. The man in front briefly knocked on the door before pushing the doors open. He pointed inside and soon after the huge doors closed leaving the man standing outside.

"We have a problem. They want urgent answers," explained the man taking off his glasses. A woman was seated in this palatial office. The office looked splendid and well decorated with picture frames and art on the walls. The woman rose from the comfy seat and walked toward the window. She looked outside without saying anything. Outside were a group of people who had gathered.

"They want to know why the senator has not addressed them up to now? Everyone needs answers right now."

"What's the update?"

"Bad."

"Out of ten."

"Twelve,"

"Damn."

"That's not all."

"What do you mean?"

The man took his time and kept quiet but walked toward the window and looked outside.

"It's a mess."

"How did this get out of control?" "Ambush. They thought?"

"I can't even comprehend this. If this is out, we are finished."

"Accidents do happen?"

"Massacre if you ask me. The scale is unrepresented. Even now more are still dying as we speak."

The woman walked to the comfy seat and sat down.

"What seemed to be the problem?"

"We can't contain it. It is left till late. I understand some victims are still alive." "Take them to the hospital but restrict visitors."

"Leaving loose ends."

"What do you have in mind?"

The woman asked before adding more. "No. I don't want any dirty hands. No." "Too late for that. Give the command. Damage limitation."

The woman slumped back on her seat and folded her hands. In the suburban area, a car sped onto the yard of one of the houses. Two men got off and ran upstairs pushing the doors until they have reached one of the bedrooms upstairs.

"Is the ambulance downstairs?" asked one of the men. One of the men who had just arrived pointed with his eyes to one of the men who were already in the house.

"No, I am not going out. Is the ambulance coming?"

"We have to carry her into the car and wait for further instructions."

CHAPTER FOUR

A Lamborghini sped into the yard of one of the mansions in the suburban area in another part of the city. The doors slowly opened and a lady wearing a saucy short red dress came out and wriggled correcting the dress and walked into the mansion. Soon after that, she was upstairs into the study room.

"You back already. What time is it?" the man looked at his watch and quickly got up.

"Any luck?"

"Not really. In fact, I haven't been trying." "What? So why did you not come to join me?"

"Something is happening over this area. There has been a lot of activity the entire day. I am picking up signals." The woman quickly looked at the big screen and walked toward the man and hugged him from the back.

"Come let's fuck right now. Come."

The woman dragged the man.

"Joe, come."

"Anita, wait. This is way too much to ignore."

"That can wait, darling. If it has been happening the complete day what can you do about it now? Nothing. Just concentrate on getting the program running. Or we are dead."

"I got to find out what is happening."

Joe sat down and started typing on the keyboard. Anita wriggled out of the sexy red dress before flicking the dress to one side with her leg and standing semi-nude. "Joe."

"Wait," replied Joe without even looking. Anita walked toward him and danced erotically in front of him semi-nude.

"Hot. But this is hotter. Give me a minute." "Hotter. Oh, forget it."

"I didn't mean it that way. I will be with you soon darling." Anita went out of the study room leaving Joe typing something. "My God. What do we have here?"

"What did you say?" shouted Anita from the bedroom.

"Come here, darling."

"Soon afterward Anita ran upstairs wearing Joe's big T-shirt and just her knickers.

"This can be the answer to all our problems," explained Joe looking at Anita who looked confused and lost. Weeks later two cars suddenly stopped outside one of the mansions and eight men got out of cars and entered the mansion spacing as they entered. A man jumped out of the window and sped off into the bushes. Two of the men suddenly knelt on their knees and opened fired. Soon after they were up and chasing the man. Into the woods, the man ran as fast as he can. The eight men followed as fast as they can too. The man being chased was Joe. He ducked and looked everywhere. The men arrived where he had been and instantly stood there in a triangle shape. Two of the men ducked to the ground landing on their knees before firing shots instantly followed by the other two men who fired at an angle to the first and the other men did the same and soon after all eight men were down on their knees facing opposite directions having fired several shots. Suddenly they all got up simultaneously, and they all cursed soon afterward.

"We need back up."

"Did you get him? I repeat did you get him?"

"No, sir."

"What do you mean no?"

"I think he escaped."

"Eight highly skilled men. Are you telling me that he got away?"

"Yes, Sir."

"Get back here now."

"We can't. Send back up."

"What?"

"Just send backup okay."

Soon afterward the line went dead. In one of the hotels, a couple were having sex. The man instantly stopped and listened.

"What is it? Don't stop," shouted the woman. The man got up and looked for the remote control and increased the volume. A news anchorwoman was on the television.

"Just in, the manager of the troubled bank had been killed today in a car accident. It is understood that he was alone when his car collided with a lorry. The police are not treating his death as suspicious he left a wife and kids. It is not known how this happened but it's a tragic loss. Mavis reporting for Touchladybirdlucky news." The man looked at the television and quickly flicked channels.

"I can't believe he is gone."

"Come back to bed."

"No, I have to go. I will call you."

The man quickly got dressed and left the hotel soon afterward. Later he was in his car driving away. He pressed the button on the car phone system.

"We have a problem. Did you hear the news? Let's meet at the bank."

"Can that wait?"

"We have to follow protocol. We must change the security codes immediately. Protocol mate."

"What can happen? It was an accident you heard it for yourself."

"Like I said protocol. Let's cover our backs okay."

"Okay let's meet at the bank."

Quickly a car parked outside one of the banks in the

city and a man got out quickly. The man walked very fast into the elevators and went upstairs. Minutes later another car parked outside. A huge man got out and entered the building slowly taking his time. The first man entered the office upstairs and sat on his desk punching on the keyboard. A quick knock on the door and the door opened. A heavy man stood at the doorway taking his breath.

"Come on in. We have to do this until we are sure it was an accident."

"Timothy relax, will you? They said it was an accident."

"Sorry to bring you here like this but we have to follow protocol."

"I understand but you sound like he was tortured first and then shot dead where the protocol comes into effect."

"I just have a bad feeling about this. Let's do this and get over with it, Okay," said Timothy getting up and pulling a chair for Darrick.

"Your passwords please." Darrick breathed heavily, and he sat on one side taking his wallet out and passing a small card to Timothy. Minutes later they had entered the main system.

"I can't seem to understand why we are losing a lot of money like that. I have a mortgage and a family mind you. We have to cover our backs in case the auditors came knocking."

"Nothing to be afraid of. We are within our scope."

"I know mate. I am just saying."

The phone interrupted the conversation. The two men looked at each other. "Protocol. We can't answer any calls while changing the password and ownership of accounts," suggested Timothy.

"Relax, will you? Are you trying to give me a heart attack? You start sounding like my doctor now. Don't do this don't do that. Relax. Jesus. They said it was an accident. Okay." Darrick searched his pockets before pulling out his phone. He answered the phone and looked at Timothy who raised his eyebrows before sinking his head into the computer.

"Listen very carefully. Don't try anything stupid. You are being robbed right now," said an automated voice leaving Darrick fuming and about to disconnect the phone. "Who is this? What do you want?" Timothy stopped for a while before carrying on with the password and account change.

"You are being robbed right now, Darrick."

"Who are you how did you know my name?" Timothy stopped and looked at Darrick.

"Are you okay?"

"Listen. Don't try anything funny let Timothy complete the password and account change first."

"Fuck you. You call this number again. I will kill you."

"I said don't try anything stupid."

"Or else what?"

Instantly Darrick put the phone down. "Quickly finish and let's go."

The sudden ringing of the cell phone sends Darrick into a panic.

"Have you finished? Let's go."

Shouted Darrick getting up. Chantelle woke up one morning and took a bath and soon after she was in the kitchen having breakfast while watching the wall television. "Two cars were involved in a collision with another car and all three men involved died two at the scene. It is understood the other men died in the hospital this morning. Unofficial reports suggest that two of the men worked in the city troubled bank and it is understood they were coming from the meeting. This bank has been manned with serious problems in recent weeks. It was just a few days ago when they lost another senior executive in a road accident as well. Although the accidents are not treated as suspicious it leaves a lot of questions unanswered. Yuri's reporting for Touchladybirdlucky news." Chantelle stopped eating and went upstairs and switched on the bedroom television and sat on the bed.

"Are you not going to work or what?"

"All three senior bosses died just days after the other."

"What? That is shocking, were they traveling together?"

Chantelle lifted the bed sheets and entered inside.

"I am scared. I can't go to work today. What are the odds of that happening?" "They work long unsocial hours don't forget that. I understand they were coming from the bank meeting."

"Exactly not from some bank party." "Either way these things do happen you know." A woman was pushed to the ground sending her bags flying in the air. Another passerby was pushed against the shop windows. A man looked everywhere scanning the whole area. He quickly crossed the road onto the other side of the pavement before he started running again. This time people were getting out of his way before he had arrived. He stopped again and scanned the entire area. A woman came out of one of the shops and ran as fast as she can. The man saw the commotion ahead and ran toward there, only stopping to scan the area. The man suddenly crossed the road onto the other side. Ahead he could see people reacting as if someone had just passed them running and pushing them. He ran as fast as he can before throwing himself to the ground landing on his knees. Quickly he withdrew his gun and fired shots looking down. Ahead shop windows were shattered and broken down one after the other. People ducked for cover. The man got up and proceeded ahead. Into the car park. On the second floor, the man stopped and threw himself down before getting up on his knees aiming his gun. He looked down and instantly fired a shot. He flipped ninety degrees and fired another shot until he had fired in all directions. Soon after a car revved so hard that the man froze with fear and got up quickly pointing the gun in all directions listening to the sound of the car. The car screeched its tires sending blue smoke into the air before it sped toward the man. In a split of a second the man jumped and flipped into the air three times before landing a distance away. The car screeched its tires to a halt before the clicking of the reverse gear was heard. The man stood there and fired some shots shattering the back window of the car before the car started reversing into his direction. Just before impact the man jumped into the air and flipped falling sideways just as the car had passed. The car stopped and instantly drove forward again narrowly missing the man, but this time headed out of the car park and into the main road leaving other drivers blasting their horns and cursing. The man knelt on his knees and listened as the car sped away.

"These bastards are after me. He nearly shot me. But I circumfucked him blind. He can't see fuck all."

"What! Get out of there."

The woman threw the cell phone on the passenger seat and drove as fast as she can, passing other cars. A huge black SUV arrived at the car park and slowly entered the driveway before coming to a halt on the upper level. A man in a suit got out of the SUV.

"You missed again."

"This one is a way out of my league. She was trained I guess."

"You are just not that good."

"As if you can do better."

"Ask the boss for me to go to your place okay."

"Just correct this and let's go."

"I can't the boss has to reset it."

"What! Weeks ago, we did reset it at the scene."

"I know."

"So."

"My friend you have a lot to learn every day you miss an opportunity. They get wiser too. Only the boss can reset it now and to be honest I think you better listen to me."

"Why is that?"

"I don't think you are worth the price of resetting it."

Whispered the other man.

"I thought it's free."

"With these mistakes, you are a liability now. Soon the boss will find it cheaper to kill you than to reset it. Be smart. I am just saying."

"Really. I was close. I should have taken her out."

"Honestly I think she deliberately left you alive."

"Na."

"You are not worth a damn even killing. You are a civilian now otherwise if you were a real threat or if she had seen you as one she could have killed you."

"I fought hard."

"She never fired at you. In that state you were in.

Death."

"Promise I will kill her next time."

"The boss might probably pay her to kill you," the man laughed.

"Hold my hand."

Soon after that the SUV hit the road and vanished. A limousine left the busy road and entered a secured building in the city. The man at the door quickly walked toward the limousine and opened the back door. A woman came out of the limo and looked around before being whisked away. The woman followed by two uniformed men walked the corridors until they have reached what looked like the reception. A woman was seated but stood instantly at the appearance of this woman.

"Ma'am."

She pointed toward the big closed door. The woman knocked at the door and waited before going inside. She came back and held the door for the woman.

"Mrs. Vice President. We have been waiting for."

"Mr. President. Thank you."

"Are you ready?"

"Ready."

They signaled the countdown before the broadcasting began.

"With much sadness, I would like to announce the death of the senator," she paused and looked straight into the camera before looking down.

"We understand his entourage was ambushed and unfortunately he was killed. The two men behind this were captured and killed too."

"But Mrs. Vice President we understand that women and children were killed as well. What do you say to that?"

Questioned one of the reporters who was seated in front. The Vice President waited for a while before addressing the question. "We believe that these men murdered the women and children to gain access to their houses to ambush the senator. Until we have a full report, we can't comment further."

"We understand that one of the men killed was the husband and father of the deceased. Can you comment on that?" The Vice President looked at the President before clearing her throat.

"We can't comment on hearsay and speculation. Until we have the full report I am afraid that's all for now."

The Vice President turned around and about to

leave when the reporters went berserk screaming and shouting. The Vice President and the President soon disappeared. Weeks after the office incident Vicky was back at work although not herself. She looked scared most of the time. Since her return, she had left her door open all the time and never closed the curtains. Often, she would invite Mart in her office. The first days were very hard for her. Every time she sat on her desk she would relive the ordeal of that day that left her scared and frightened. Often, she would get up and sometimes go out of the office altogether. Ever since her return, she had worn heavy clothing and never the saucy sexy silk dresses. Very often she would ask silly questions just to get Mart and Tim's attention to talk to them or just have company. Tim couldn't stop laughing at her when it was only him and Mart. Mart felt pain every time he looked at her and the way she was that day. Surely something bad had happened to her. This time she would fight any urges she had and sometimes she murmured vulgar words to control the urges that at one point after hearing her curse Tim thought that she had turrets. Mart looked at her as she spoke to herself.

"Is she on the phone?"

"Leave her alone. It's not funny anymore." "Look Mr. Lover boy pretending to care." "She changed man. Look ever since returning she never closed her office door." Tim burst into laughter startling her as she overhead him laugh.

"Actually, it is good for you, Mart! Just imagine other doors not closed too. Hey." "Stop it. Can you be sensitive?"

"Don't talk to me like that. I saw what they were doing that day."

"Not your business. Something bad happened. I am going to talk to her."

"I can't stop you. Go."

Mart got up and knocked on the door.

"It's open. Of course, you can see that. What can I do for you?"

"Talk," said Mart pushing the door.

"No. Please don't close the door," shouted Vicky so loud that Tim looked at them and shook his head.

"You seemed agitated and scared lately. You okay?"

"Don't worry about me, let's just say it's a female thing," Mart kept quiet for some time and smiled.

"Ah, that makes sense. I was worried about you. I thought something bad had happened to you that day." Vicky looked down and quickly had a flashback of her hand rubbing her pussy. Strong erotic feelings rushed down her spine to her clitoris setting her on fire that she quickly closed her legs making things worse that she instantly opened her legs and at the same time felt like something was oozing out from between her legs.

"Bad. Evil. Bastards. Bitch. Whore," whispered Vicky but loud enough for Mart to have heard.

"What?"

"Oh no. Nothing to do with you. I am just thinking out loud. So, what do you want to talk about?"

"What happened that day? I still can picture you."

"Drop it. It's past I don't want to talk about it."

"See. You are hiding something from me. I know more than you think," Vicky stopped what she was doing and sat comfortably resting back on the seat before quickly closing her eyes and then looking at Mart. "What are you saying?"

"A lot more happened that day than you are telling."

"Just because you saw me with my knickers down that can't give you a reason to interrogate me. Okay. I have better things to do."

"We all know that?"

"What is that supposed to mean? Listen. Get that dirty thought out from your head. Just because you

saw me like that doesn't mean you can try to
blackmail me into fucking you. Okay. Get out!"

"No. No. No, it's not like that."

"What? You don't want to fuck me? What are you
saying?"

"No. Yes. I mean. Listen."

OK, I am listening. Go ahead."

"What else happened that day? Did you get hacked?
I mean did the system got hacked?" Vicky looked
worried and scared that she got up and walked
toward the door and closed it. She walked behind
Mart and stopped as Tim looked on. She knelt and
hugged Mart from behind and kissed him on the
cheek all this time Tim was watching. Then she
walked toward the side windows and pulled the
curtain closed. Mart looked surprised as blood
suddenly rushed where he did not expect it to. Once
the curtain closed Vicky walked to her chair and sat
down.

"Just for him so that he doesn't ask unwanted
questions," suddenly Mart's face dropped down.

"What seemed to be the problem? It's just for him
so that he stops giving you the sticks. I sometimes
hear you fighting over me. That's very sweet but
listen very carefully. What happened that day stays
in here and never leaves this room okay. I have a

reputation to keep."

"I am talking about the system."

"What do you mean?" Mart leaned forward.

"Only your office had Internet access. Only your computer was running. Are you and your boyfriend up to something and trying to stage this sex act?"

"Oh my God. How many times must I suffer before someone started believing me? Jesus!"

"Because you are not telling me the truth even Tim knows the Internet to your office was on. It must be something huge for you to throw that flashing act."

"Mart, what do you want?"

"Don't get me wrong I am not blackmailing you. No. But I am a concerned friend surely something more is going on than you are telling me."

"Jesus! They set me up."

Shouted Vicky slumping on her back-chair rest. She looked at Mart and realized that this was never going to go away. Instantly she had a flashback of that day especially that message she had seen. Surely a bigger force was there to get her. She never looked at it from that angle. Either way, if Mart can't believe her then surely no one will.

"Okay. I was horny. You know this thing with David, so I gave myself a quickie no big deal."

"Okay but the port access was active don't tell me you can juggle."

Vicky looked upset and got up as she became aroused but scared as well. "Maybe someone hacked the system."

"Bullshit. No one can access the system that way. Only you can. Even myself I cannot."

"I don't know. Honestly, I don't know." "What is with this flashing act? I think it will be hard to convince anyone otherwise. It looked like you had planned all this to cover for tampering with the system. Is David part of this?"

"Leave him out of this. He had nothing to do with this."

"Protecting him, huh? I think he is the mastermind."

Vicky walked toward the window and looked outside and started crying.

"He left me. I told him what happened. He couldn't believe me. He thought that something was going on."

Mart stood up and walked toward her and hugged her.

"He left you just because of that?"

Vicky cried like a baby. She placed her head on Mart's shoulder. The area between her legs was on fire it has been weeks since someone touched her there. She felt like exploding in every sense of the word. Surely that thing that had jumped into her was still inside her setting her on fire with each passing day. It was just unbearable. The turrets cursing was not helping either. Whatever had jumped into her that day was still inside her giving her intense arousal but the fear of what happened after that would erase these feelings instantly. "David was very scared. He said that whoever was behind this was going to eliminate everyone I have told."

"Oh. Smart guy."

Said Mart as the blood that had built up in his pants suddenly vanished. Mart looked worried too.

"Hey if nothing was stolen then everything should be okay. I guess."

Vicky did not reply but started squeezing Mart and kissing him passionately. This is what Mart had waited forever since he laid eyes on her but somehow it felt very wrong. He couldn't even make any of his blood warm enough. He was like a dog that had seen a ghost with a tail of fear between its legs rather than the usual waving tail. It was weeks since David had left. Fear and a sense of insecurity had driven her mad, but she just couldn't contain the feelings. She immediately stabbed Mart with her tongue and Mart could feel all her tongue in his mouth. He struggled to take it out before he asked.

"Do you think this is a clever idea?"

Vicky looked at him and quickly took her knickers off but first after checking that she was still logged onto the system. She unfastened his belt and lowered his trousers before rubbing his private parts. Mart stood there unbelieving his eyes. He felt like this was a dream. Soon after that, he felt Vicky stroking and sucking his manhood. This was it. Although this is what he had waited for it felt wrong. The more he thought about it the more blood rushed up to his brain than down where it should have been and the more, he felt Vicky pulling and licking. She knelt and pulled her long dress up before she started stroking her pussy wild and with the other hand, she squeezed hard one of her breasts whilst pleasuring Mart. That was the catalyst. Mart had a flashback of that day and quickly felt warm blood running down his private parts. He held Vicky's arm and lifted her up and placed his tongue in her mouth squeezing hard her breasts before lifting her high up and instantly she hooked her legs around his waist and placed her arms around his neck and ride him very fast. Mart instantly placed his hands on her buttocks and jerked her up and down very hard until she started making orgasmic moans. A red BMW M8 cruised on the road heading away from the city. The driver looked agitated as he drove the car. He slammed hard the steering wheel before making a U-turn in the road and suddenly stopping. A Carolinadeivid song was playing, Angels and Hot lips. He stopped as if listening to the song before revving the sports car and driving off leaving a lot of smoke on the road. After a while, he knelt to pick up his cell phone that had dropped down and when he raised his head, he saw what appeared to be a man kneeling in the middle of the road. Instantly he applied the brakes and held firm the steering wheel. The car skidded and for some strange reason the man looked unmoved as he remained kneeling in the middle of the road. David blasted the horn losing control of the car as it meandered in the road. A few feet away David swerved the car narrowly missing the man before the car hit the metal guide on the roadside. The car bonnet suddenly opened and hot water started coming out of the carburetor and smoke from the screeching tires covered the whole road. David got out of the car coughing as smoke was choking him. He took his breath and walked to the place where the man once knelt, but he was gone. He stood there and looked around. After the smoke had cleared the man reappeared standing in the middle of the road ahead of him. Instantly the man threw himself down before kneeling on his knees in the middle of the road and instantly withdrew a gun and fired shots while looking downward. One bullet pierced David's flesh but not bad enough to cause any major bleeding. He soon ducked before running for his life. The man followed him and after a while would duck and on his knees, would fire shots at David. He would get up and chased after him. The chase continued before David reached an open area and stood there. He looked around before he disappeared in the surrounding bushes. The man followed and waited in the open area and instantly he took cover before getting up on his knees and scanned the area with his eyes closed just listening to the sound. He aimed in all directions and fired shots. A few seconds later a scream echoed a mile away. The man smiled and got up.

"I got you."

Before walking in the direction, the noise had come from. As he arrived, he knelt and looked at fresh blood. He had just wounded him. He looked around for blood drops before heading in one direction looking down.

"Lost something?"

Asked David behind the man at a distance away. The man flipped three times in the air before landing on a new position David had instantly fired a bullet missing the man and getting another one on the shoulder instead. The man smiled before getting up and walking toward David who lay down holding his shoulder.

"What do you want from me? Who are you?"

"I am the man you saved on the road and the man

who is going to kill you."

"What? But I have just saved your life." "Either way I am still going to kill you." "What if I had knocked you down?"

"You don't have the guts. You run away from that woman. You left us with no choice but to kill you both quickly,"
"What? You bastard. If you touch her, I will kill you. I swear, leave her out of this."
"Your choice. We created a situation wherein the end we get what we want. A situation where you are the driver. Where you decide your destiny."

"I don't understand. You just said you were going to kill us both."

"Yes. But the first option was better. A win-win for everyone."

"How come?"

"See Mr. we hooked her and elevated all her senses but the senses of knowing when to stop. We created a situation where she lived just for sex. Everything around her will be about sex. We know she already told you what happened at the bank? In the end, we would say she stole the money to fund her drug habit?"

"But she is not on drugs. She will never touch that stuff."

"I know that's when you come in. Were you not banging your head on the steering wheel?"

"Still that does not make any sense." "Don't forget the sex bit."

"And."

"In the end, we were going to say that you have a big dick and that you caused her brain damage."

"What? Who would believe such a stupid thing?"

"We would say that you fucked her brains out literally."

"Please. Are you fucked up or what?"

"Soon or later she won't resist. She is right now screwing that boy. What's his name? Mart. We created a situation wherein the end they will fuck until they get caught. We will use Tim. He has already seen her behaving like a madwoman. We will still say they have stolen the money and spend the money on drugs and the drugs caused the brain damage and whatever she said is therefore not credible. But you chose death. Honestly, we would not want you dead. No. We don't mind you walking around with one or two long nails in your brain."

"I spared your life. Let her go. Let us go." "Thank you, that's why I will let you die a slow death. Give you time to say your last rituals."

"Bastard. I should have killed you."

"In your dreams," said the man before flipping in the air several times before landing on David's wounded shoulder. He screamed and growled in pain.

"I shot you with my eyes closed."

"What are you? What's with this kneeling in the middle of the road?"

"I said say your last rituals."

"Son of a bitch." David instantly pulled a gun. The man looked at David and smiled. "Still you haven't learned anything. Okay. Get up. Die like a man."

The man started walking in a straight line away from David. David looked surprised but quickly got up and aimed his gun. The man walked for a while and stopped and knelt as soon as David had fired a shot. Instinctively David flipped to the side anticipating the man to flip and fire at him. He flipped twice and landed on the right side of his previous position. At the same time, the man had flipped into the air and fired a shot before he touched the ground. David looked at himself. The man had fired in the wrong direction, to the left side.

"Your last rituals."

"Fuck off you missed. You thought I would jump to the left. What are you?"

"I never miss."

"You just did."

"Geo-locational correction. I am going to shoot you with my eyes closed."

David looked around and thought quickly before he started running in a circle circulating the man. The man threw himself onto the ground before getting up on his knees and firing consecutive shots before hearing a thump. The man stood up but instantly cursed and stopped. David looked on as he tried to stop the bleeding on his collar bone. The pain was unbearable that he couldn't talk. The man walked without raising his head and stopped and listened first before walking toward David. David realized that something was wrong. Was this a human being or what? He slowly fought the pain and stretched his arm before holding still. The man stopped and listening and urged forward. When he was in shooting range David pulled the trigger.

CHAPTER FIVE

A drone lifted from a house and into the air. It flew over the suburbs, over the plains and mountains and over the river. Whilst flying over the river the drone swerved from left to right as it flew at very low altitude. Instantly an eagle came from nowhere and chased after the drone.

"Oh, we have company!" shouted Anita. "What is it?" asked Joe from the shower room.

"Why can't you come and see for yourself." Joe came out of the shower and quickly doused the water and wore the big robe. "Lose that quickly," shouted Joe.

"Watch this." Anita held the joystick with both hands and flew the drone looking at the big screen in the bedroom.

"What are you trying to do?"

"Lose the eagle-like you said."

"Think like a bird. If it's a bird, it will definitely swerve and make sharp turns because it has no chance with the eagle." "That's what I am trying to do."

On the big screen, the cameras on the drone showed the eagle following the drone. Anita had tried to escape the eagle, but the eagle was very persistent. The drone flew over the river and into the surrounding forests. At one time the eagle had tried to grab it but failed. That was the closest it has been. "I think I have to lose the cargo otherwise we are going to lose everything." "Then go back to the river and drop it in the river."

"Then what's the point that way we won't get any pictures. We will just be feeding them."

"It's better that way. We still have the drone. We can launch again."

"I have an idea to give me. Let me fly the drone." Joe jumped onto the bed and took the drone remote joystick.

"Watch how it's done."

The eagle flew on top of the drone for a while then quickly lost height flipping upside down as it reached the bottom of the drone where the big price was. Its long claws grabbed the juicy duck that was being carried by the drone and instantly Joe lowered the drone so fast that the eagle thought that it was going to crash down that it released the duck and instantly Joe lifted the drone and its cargo. The eagle looked like it was floating in the air upside down before flipping 180 degrees and resumed the chase. Joe flew the drone to the river and flew the drone at a very low level. The eagle instead flew upward and circled the drone from above. Instantly it dropped free falling at lightning speed and flipped upside down and instantly grabbed the duck that was underneath the drone Joe instantly dropped the drone on top of the eagle and the duck that the drone's weight pushed the eagle into the water. Fearing for itself the eagle released its claws and freed the duck. Immersed in water the eagle flapped its wings and was about to fly when the piranhas in the river jumped out of the water and went after the eagle and back into the water. Instantly there was a feeding frenzy. The piranhas came from nowhere and in seconds they were tearing the duck apart removing chunks of flesh. The eagle flapped its wet wings and tried to fly out of the water first time but failed. Then on a second trial, it flipped its wings and raised slightly above the water. As soon as its legs were clear of the river water, some piranhas jumped out of the water and tore away chunks of flesh from the eagle. In seconds the piranhas did what they do best. The piranhas wriggled very hard as they tore chunks of flesh. Soon the water turned red with blood. All this time the drone was recording the footage. Anita and Joe looked at each other.

"Oh my God."

In seconds the duck and the eagle had been mauled. The piranhas attacked several times in seconds one attack after the other tearing chunks of flesh. The fish would wriggle in a flash and disappear but return in a fraction of a second.

"Let's look at the footage again."

"So, I think I will be able to complete the program." Joe got up and took his laptop and started programming formulas and simulations.

"If piranhas can eat away large chunks of flesh in seconds, we can extract copious amounts in seconds without sending shock shaves as well."

"Why previous programs crashed?"

"I think I took each transaction as a separate occurrence and all combined these caused the system to crash. But now I think the answer is to view every transaction as part of the whole entity." "Sure. Although the eating habits look random and frenzy, I think the piranhas communicate. Look at this, they swim at lightning speeds surely if that was random they would collide and kill each other." "True, I think they communicate with each other somehow they pass static electric currents." For the next weeks, Joe fully developed the program. Miles away a car parked outside a huge mansion. Four men got out of the car and waited outside the huge gates. Soon after they entered the yard of the house. Four huge black dogs with amputated tails came running toward them and stood in front of them.

"Is the boss going to feed us to the dogs." "You always make stupid jokes."

One of the dogs barked at the man who was talking.

"Oh, oh maybe you are right."

The door opened. A woman came out of the house.

"In the house!"

The dogs ran into the house.

"The boss is expecting you.

" The men entered the house.

"I don't understand why you can't carry out a simple task."

"It's not easy. Somehow he is trapping us." "You must find a way out of this."

"We are trying to boss."

"He double-crossed me. I think he wants to sell the

technology to other people."

"Can he do that?"

"The deal was that that technology was just for me."

"So, what happened?"

"I tried to get him murdered."

"What I don't understand is why the universe is controlled and getting robbed by the smallest person possible. He is just 22 years."

"I want all the software, or he will end up like his father."

A blue Lamborghini revved in the road before coming to a halt in the city. Joe got out of the car and entered the bank headquarters. He entered the elevator and went to the offices above.

"How can I help?"

"I am here to see the bank's CEO."

"Yes, he is expecting you. Come this way." Joe followed the secretary to a well-decorated office with gold-coated walls and exotic furniture.

"Wait here he will be with you soon."

Joe looked around admiring the trophy and

memorabilia. He could feel the comfy carpet as he strolled into the office. He walked to the other wall showing all previous chief executives and admired them all.

"Mr. Joe, I am the CEO. Call me Fabian. Shall we?"

"My father left me a lot of money and I would like to invest in your bank I am talking about $billions."

"I understand Mr. Joe have you talked to our investment managers they can help you invest that money."

"Mr. Fabian, I am looking to be part of your banking group if that means buying shares. I see you have a bigger brighter future. I heard you are one of the best in the field."

"That's what they say but honestly I do what comes naturally to me. I can only say I am gifted and experienced."

"I see this company has a good long-term strategy and what is your area of strength as a business, so I assess my best investment opportunities?"

"I think investment portfolios are doing very well. You know what just hold on I have someone I would like you to meet." The CEO reached for the phone and dialed a number.

"So how much are you willing to invest Mr. Joe?"

"$1 billion."

"Very nice."

A knock at the door startled Joe and Fabian.

"Come in," shouted Fabian.

A beautiful blonde lady with a very long dress came in.

"Vicky meet Mr. Joe. Our client. He wants to assess investment opportunities."

Vicky looked at Joe and walked toward where he was sitting. As she approached, Joe briefly glanced between her legs and she instantly stopped and sneezed so hard that she felt like she had had an orgasm as well. It felt like the day she gave herself a quickie in the office. Joe licked his lips before he got up to greet her. He stretched his hand and when he touched her hand, she instantaneously closed her legs together and squeezed the area between her legs. Her eyelids blinked several times before she let out another sneeze.

"Are you okay Vicky? I will leave you two to get acquainted when you have decided Mr. Joe then come and see me."

"Oh, No Sir. I can't."

Vicky looked at Fabian.

"You are the Managing director of Investment banking how can you say you can't?"

"Mart or Tim will be ideal."

"Don't bring your personnel issues to work. He is our client. I want you to show him all the investment portfolios," Fabian looked surprised and sounded upset.

"OK talk in my office. I will be back after an hour. I want to know the outcome of this meeting. Be good to him."

Fabian looked at Vicky and left the office leaving Joe and Vicky.

"So, you are very choosy, huh? Or I just look too young to be taken seriously? Oh, let me see. You are used to old clients that way you have the opportunity to fuck them too."

"You, cheeky bastard I know it was you." "Me what? We just met. I have never seen your face before. So please let's get down to business."

"You bastard. If you wanted the money why didn't you get just the money?" "Why?"

"Why what? As if you didn't enjoy it."

"Son of a bitch. I want you to take it out. I can't

think. I am scared all the time."

"I have to lick you to remove it."

"If I had a gun, I will kill you myself."

"I can get you one if you like."

"You think this is funny. Maybe I call the police."

Joe took out his phone and put it on the table.

"Go ahead. And say what? That you stole the money with your boyfriend and that he ran away with the money. Or say that something is making you very horny, and it's between your legs. In that case, they might say remove that vagina and buy yourself a dick instead. That's the only explanation that makes sense."

"What do you want?"

"I came here to do business like any other client why do you have to be such a pain?" "I will give you five minutes to leave me alone. Tell the boss you are not interested or else I am going to tell him the truth. Or I will go to the police."

"How are you going to get there?" Said Joe before smiling cheekily.

"What?" Vicky looked shocked and scared that her voice patterns supported this. "Son of a bitch. I am going to kill you. It was you too."

"If you can see me yeah then your lucky chance."

"OK what do you what?" said Vicky sitting down frightened.

"I want to be the CEO of this bank from today." "Excuse me."

"You heard me."

"Are you out of your fucking mind? We have a CEO already. It's not something you can do overnight. You have to be qualified."

"Wrong."

"What? Do you think you can get away with this?"

"Who will stop me? The CEO Mr. Fabian? Come here I want to show you something." Joe walked to the window of the big office and looked outside before looking at Vicky. "Look below on the road what do you see?" Vicky looked quickly before looking back at Joe. "Just cars. Listen I don't want to play any games."

"Trust me it's not a game. Look again." Vicky looked quickly this time more scared.

"Nothing. You know what? I am going." Joe grabbed Vicky by the waist and pushed her against the window.

"Look down. OK look up there. What do you see? Look very carefully. Something red. Something fast. Now, look at the road in front of you."

"No. What are you trying to do? No. No. You bastard."

A red sports car drove at high speed as soon as Fabian entered the road. Vicky looked at the car and then at Fabian fearing the worst then at the car and then at Fabian as the gap closes.

"Get out of the road. Walk fast. Go. Go. Go," shouted Vicky looking outside the window from the top floor. Suddenly Fabian stopped in the middle of the road. "What is he doing? Why are you stopping? Go. Move!" shouted Vicky.

"Fabian! Get out of the road! OMG!"

The red sports car increased its speed when it was near Fabian. Fabian for some strange reasons remained standing in the road even though the car was coming his way. The car hit him at a fast speed sending him flying in the air before he hit the ground very hard. Vicky covered her face and cried and soon after ran outside the office. Joe looked through the window. Soon after a crowd started gathering as Fabian lay on the ground with blood coming from his nostrils, ears, and mouth. Vicky ran across the road and knelt to check if Fabian was still alive. She quickly covered her mouth and looked at Fabian's office window and saw Joe stood there. Joe looked down and pointed in the direction the car came from and quickly Vicky got up and ran back to the office building. She pushed the doors and ran to the elevators and pressed the buttons so fast before taking the stairs. She was breathing heavily and crying. Stairs after stairs she went up. On the top floor, she pushed Fabian's office door very hard.

"Son of a bitch. Remove this now. Where are you?" She searched everywhere, but the office was deserted. Joe was nowhere to be seen. Weeks after that Vicky entered the conference room. A lot of people were seated around the table. She looked around at everyone and remembered most of the people. The shareholders, the managers, and all the investors. She looked in front and saw only two seats empty. She reached for one of the seats and sat down.

"Where is he?" Vicky looked at everyone and smiled. She instantly placed her legs together and briefly closed her eyes.

"He is coming. He is here." Instantly the doors opened. Vicky got up.

"Ladies and gentlemen. I introduce you to the new CEO, Mr. Joe."

Everyone looked at him. Instantly there was a huge

buzz as the people started talking to each other.

"I would like to say. I was appointed after the auditors found out that Mr. Fabian was embezzling money from the bank. So be rest assured that I will look after your money and as the majority shareholder, where the CEO suddenly dies, I become overseer until the board of directors has found a replacement. So, shall we?" Joe strolled around the conference table.

"How tragic life can be? How vulnerable we humans are. You wake up one day and the next minute you are dead. That brings me to another question. How much value can you put on your life?" Joe looked at everyone as they all looked at each other. "Priceless. I should say."

"How much is your life worth?" No one answered that they all looked at each other. "OK, how much can you exchange for your life?"

"OK let me put it this way, how much can you give to secure your life? How much of what you have can you exchange for your life?"

Everyone looked at each other.

"Ladies and gentlemen. I want you to think hard about this question. How much of what you have today can you give in exchange for your life? I want you all to take a piece of paper in front of you." Joe looked at Vicky who instantly got up and placed a piece of paper on everyone's table. "I want you to write down how much you think your life is worth as a fraction of your net worth. Be honest because I am going to write down next to your figure how much I think each one of you deserve, let us say we stop doing business today. Trust me no one will see each other's figure, but you will all see mine." Mr. Zhang got up and looked upset.

"Is this a game? I don't have time for all this."

"Mr.?"

"Zhang. Mr. Zhang."

"Yes. Mr. Zhang. So, I assume that your life is worth all what you have invested with this bank and all your private accounts in Hong Kong and in Japan. Let me see that comes to $300 million. Oh, I mean $370 million including the Swiss accounts." Mr. Zhang instantly took out his pocket calculator and calculated it quickly. He looked at Joe with an astonished and frightened face.

"How did you know that?"

"Sit down Mr. Zhang." Joe strolled to the front of the table.

"I want everyone to be honest. I ask you to write down a fraction or amount you will be willing to give to secure your life. This is just an exercise. The death of Mr. Fabian no matter how bad he was, has raised some fundamental questions." Joe sat comfortably in his chair.

"Once you have written a value turn the paper upside down. I will come around and write the value this bank will give you just to secure your life."

Everyone looked at each other and after that, they all started writing on the small pieces of papers only to be interrupted by Joe.

"One more thing so it's fair, I want you to close your eyes after you have written your value and turned the paper upside down. Okay?"

Vicky glanced at Joe with wide-opened eyes. Joe cunningly smiled and sat comfortably in his chair. Vicky did not write anything but instead kept staring at Joe.

"If you have finished please do as I said turn the paper upside down and then close your eyes. Okay?"

"OK," answered every one. Joe stood up and walked around the conference table looking at the figures before writing another figure next to it. After he had finished, he sat down comfortably. Vicky all this time was just sat there looking at Joe.

"I agree with most of you that nearly 90% of you would give nearly all your fortune to preserve your life. Joe stood up and walked toward Mr. Zhang.

"Mr. Zhang. Why do you think that only 20% of your net worth is the only amount you will give to secure your life? I thought your life is worth more than money. Priceless. For most, they would rather give all their money to secure life. Why don't you?"

"Simple. I inherited 80% of the fortune and technically this belongs to my kids and future generations. I will only give what I have earned myself."

"Okay. Who else thinks like Mr. Zhang?" "Mrs.?"

"Penguin."

"Yes, Mrs. Penguin."

"I would not give anything at all. My life is priceless. So, I am safer if I don't attach any monetary value to it. In other words, I don't give anything. Would rather die." "Interesting. Mrs. Penguin. Do you have any kids?"

"Why I need kids? All my money will go to charities when I die. I have written a will already. So, I can't give any."

"Clever Mrs. Penguin."

Joe walked back and sat down.

"Okay, I want all of you now to open your eyes and see how close you were in matching what the bank would give for your lives."

Suddenly a huge buzz filled the whole conference room.

"What's going on?"

"Who is doing this?"

"Stop it right now."

"Listen very carefully. I think all of you are not taking me seriously, especially Mrs. Penguin. I want you all to think hard about my question and match the figure I have written down. If you can see the figure. Can anyone see the figure I have written down?"

"Son of a bitch!"

"Bastard!"

"Satan!"

"Devil!"

"Bloody thief!"

"Silence, please! I will ask you again. How much is your life worth?"

"Daylight robbery. I am not giving you anything." Joe breathed heavily.

"For those who want to live, today I shall take the money you have written down from your accounts plus a 25% commission of your total value with immediate effect. No informing any authorities or anyone for that matter or your families will be enrolled in this program as well. Understood?"

"Vicky will pass around papers for you to sign authorizing the immediate transfer of the money you have written down plus fees. Failure to sign will result in termination of the contract which can result in loss of your life. Trust me if Fabian was here today, he would tell you all to sign and live your life."

"I am not going to be part of this you Bastard," shouted Vicky getting up angry and very upset. Calmly and cunningly replied Joe.

"Vicky, they all know."

"Know what?"

"That you stole the money and set up Fabian. The time the money was stolen Fabian was abroad on vacation only that you didn't know that."

"Lying Bastard."

"Your choice. Pass around the papers or let's call

the police."

"One day I will kill you myself."

"Stop complaining. You have a job and soon you will have $millions in your account."

"I don't want the money."

"OK, I will remove that thing between your legs."

Everyone stopped what they were doing and looked in the direction the voice came from, surprised and shocked.

"Oh my God. Just for the money. I will sign," shouted Mrs. Penguin.

"What are you waiting for? Pass the papers around." A man walked out of the big city-building and onto the pavement before he stopped and scanned the area. He walked to the car parked outside and opened the car door and looked everywhere. He entered the car and drove away. He drove for a while before he looked in the rear-view mirror and noticed that a car was following him. At first, he brushed the idea aside and drove for a while. He looked in the rear-view mirror again but this time the car was not following. He looked again and instantly his cell phone rang startling him. He looked to the road ahead before looking for the earpiece.

"On my way. Got a tail though."

"Lose it, damn it."

"Will try."

"Not good enough. Damn. Get rid of whoever it is. What am I paying you for?" "OK boss."

Dimitri drove as fast as he can frequently looking back to see if the car was still following him. He drove for a while before he saw that car again. Quickly he turned into a side road leaving the other drivers blasting their horns at him. As soon as he had turned into the other road, another quick glance in his rear-view mirror revealed the other car turning as well following him. His heart started beating very fast. Another quick glance in the rear-view mirror and suddenly he heard a sharp horn blast from the oncoming traffic as he had encroached into the other lane. He quickly swerved back into his lane. Another quick glance revealed the car still following this time faster. He concentrated on the road ahead increasing speed and changing gears quickly before another phone call sends him into a panic.

"The boss wants to know when you will be here."

"Got company. Can't seem to lose the tail."
"Probably that woman again. She is going to kick your ass again."

Replied Pavel laughing mockingly. "Probably not."

"You make me laugh. You are an assassin, yet you are the hunted."

"I will kill her this time."

"Tell me where you are. I will come there now."

"I can handle this."

Dimitri upset and feeling a little self-pity but determined to get the job done abruptly ended the call. He opened the glove compartment and took out the back-up gun. He drove the car very fast and quickly screeching the car tires skidding before making a U-turn in the road. The car came to a halt. He held the steering wheel revving the car in the middle of the road. Dimitri looked ahead facing the oncoming car. He noticed that there was only one person in the approaching car he felt relaxed a little but disappointed that it was not the woman he had anticipated. Somehow his heart started beating very fast. Fear struck him instantly that he thought of making another U-turn and run for his life. Immediately he recalled Pavel's words that he was the hunted. He revved the car in a rage. Bravely he got out of the car and hid the back-up gun on his back. The other man got out of his car as well but much slower and straightened his suit. Dimitri threw himself on the ground before kneeling on his knees and fired consecutive shots. Instantly the man flipped from left to right dodging the bullets before he returned fire once on his last landing nearly hitting Dimitri. Dimitri got up his heart nearly exploding with fear. Surely this man was good if not better than him. He opened the car door and about to enter inside when the man laughed and spoke.

"Pussy! Running away already."

The man threw his gun away and removed his suit jacket.

"Die like a man."

Dimitri closed the car door instantly his phone started ringing. He looked at the phone screen and saw that the call was from Pavel. He took the phone and was about to answer it when the man interrupted.

"One on one. Die like a man."

Dimitri looked at the cell phone as it kept ringing and finally threw the phone on the driver's seat and walked toward the man. The man circled Dimitri with clenched fists. Dimitri swerved clockwise 180 degrees with his right leg raised hitting the man in the face sending him tumbling to the ground. That gave him the needed confidence. He remembered training with Pavel. That was Pavel's trademark kick. The man didn't see it coming. He got up and gazed at Dimitri hesitantly. Dimitri, once he sensed fear he attacked viciously. The man was on the ground again. He got up and held the man's arms before attacking but the man quickly exchanged blows with Dimitri. Dimitri smiled before walking away a few steps. The man advanced before getting hit in the face. The man stumbled but attacked back as fast as he can, punching Dimitri in the face before the man pinched the middle neck of Dimitri. Dimitri stumbled and felt heavy blows to the face. He stumbled as he got kicked in the ribs then the head sending him to the ground. He opened his eyes but couldn't see the man. "Damn it." He cursed while nursing the wounds on his head. He felt a heavy blow to his chest and a kick in the stomach before hitting the ground. Instantly he was stampeded on. He got up and knelt before pulling the gun at his back and firing consecutive shots as fast as he can, staring down. The man he was fighting flipped in the air landing on his left before quickly jumping up again landing on his right like a cat on fire. Instantly Dimitri felt a sense of fear running down his spine before he aimed his gun away from the man and instantly fired a shot.

"You are good."

"Cheating bastard. You are not alone."

"No back up two bullets left. Look at how many we are."

"Son of a bitch."

"Oh, sorry you can't see."

Dimitri still on his knees scanned the area with his head looking down.

"Five of you."

"Oh, you are good."

"Who are you? What do you want?"

"Let's just say we are here to take you and your mates out of business. In fact, out of your misery."

"Who do you work for?"

"Not important."

Dimitri rolled onto the ground and fire a shot and flipped and then fire another one landing near the car. On the other side, two men simultaneously flipped into the air. All the five-men walked in the middle of the road and looked at Dimitri.

"Last bullets. I circumfucked him blind."
"Cowards."

"Is he that slow?"

"No, it's not him. They are still using the obsolete version."

"And he has no backup?"

"He thought he had big balls he can handle us."

"He tricked me. One on one remember."

"I lied, and you must die."

The other man pulled a gun and aimed at Dimitri.

"No. No. He must die a slow death. Allow me, let us see how good he really is."

The man approached Dimitri, and a fight broke out. They exchanged fists for a while before the other men started joining in whenever their friend was losing. Dimitri wished Pavel was there. He wished he had called him. He wished he had answered his call. Pavel was like a big brother to him. He had always been there for him. They had locked his system, mouse-trapped him blind, he couldn't see, and it required unlocking. Pavel had trained him to fight blind. It was unfair he thought. They were too many. His chances of surviving were very slim. Even if he could run away, there was nowhere he can go. He could not drive. The only thing that made his heart beat faster was the fear of being shot cowardly. There were too many. After a struggle, he started receiving lethal blows one after the other. He would run for it only to bump into something or being kicked from the back and sides. His concentration was reduced. They were too many to do anything. He fought the best he can, punching back but most of the time he could only punch the air as well as receiving punches. Exhausted and feeling his energies drained he knelt and listened only to the kicked in the head before feeling the weight of a person on his chest. He heard fading voices as some men started walking away. Instantly he heard a man breathing fast and close to his head. He felt the barrel of a gun against his head and he instinctively closed his eyes before feeling a strange feeling and splashes of water on his face. A car suddenly stopped in the parking space outside a huge building. The door flung wide open, and a woman put her legs out before getting out of the car and running into the building. She soon left the elevators and entered the conference room. The President was addressing a large crowd of journalists and reporters and other officials. There was a lot of flash photography before the President looked straight into the camera and addressed the nation. After he had finished talking and when it was question time a lady among the journalists raised her hand before the President pointed at her. She got up and held her microphone closer to her mouth. "Mr. President. Even though the Independent inquiry commissioner concluded as your government that the men killed were the men who murdered the senator. Would you murder your wife and your son just to stop certain laws from being passed?" There was a huge buzz followed by instant silence as the President raised his arms. "I can't answer for these men. We did what was required of us. I think it's time we move on."

"Mr. President is it not true also or likely that your men mistakenly shot innocent women and children the day the senator was shot dead in retaliation?"

"My men are innocent. The independent inquiry has cleared them of any wrongdoings."

The people looked at the lady to see what she was going to say next.

"I believe the government somehow assassinated the senator and killed innocent women and children and then their husbands to cover up. One of the men presumed to have killed the senator was miles away when that happened. What do you say to that?"

The President threw a quick glance at one of his bodyguards and he got the message. The bodyguard walked toward the woman and advised her to save the questions for later.

"No, I will not stop seeking the truth. Your government assassinated my brother. He was innocent. He would never kill his wife and son. He disliked politics. I have proof that he was miles away. Only to return and be gunned down by your men in cold blood."

The crowd astonished and surprised all looked at the lady with the reporters and photographers taking pictures.

"If you have personal issues, I can address them please come and see me after the meeting otherwise the conference is over." Max looked at the lady and quickly approached her.

"I am Max. I am sorry about your brother somehow it doesn't add up. These men don't fit the profile of murderers there is a lot the government is not telling us."

The lady sobbed for a while.

"I am sure he was innocent. He would never kill even a fly. They set him up. Why would he kill the senator? It doesn't make any sense."

"I believe you. Do you know that the senator was shot eight times?"

"There were no bullet casings found in the house. Were they?"

"This is the big fuck up. Listen to this. There was only one bullet casing found in the house."

"But why there was no gun found in the house if he was the shooter?"

"The initial report had no mention of any bullet casings found. They assumed the man ran for it after killing the woman and the kid. But the initial reports implied that the senator's bodyguards fired the fatal shots."

"I believe he is innocent."

"It doesn't just stop there. The gun found, guess what?"

"What?"

"Was registered government property exactly the type carried by the senator's bodyguards."

"What are you saying?"

"If you are saying that your brother was not even there then the only plausible explanation is that one of them did it and planted the gun there."

"But why? Who benefits from all this?" "That my dear. I don't know."

"Some say they instinctively retaliated after the senator was shot I presume by one of his men. The other bodyguards then opened fire at the surrounding houses. Killing women and children."

"Still it doesn't explain the chasing and why they planted the gun and how my brother ended up dead in that house when he was not even there."

"I think you should come with me let's go somewhere private."

"I have to talk to the President."

"He is just going to lie to you and confuse you even more. Talk to him later. Come." Max and Clara left the conference room and into Max's car and drove off. The car arrived at a house in the nearby suburbs and the two entered the house.

"Coffee or tea."

"Tea two sugars."

Max disappeared into the kitchen leaving Clara looking at the newspaper- cuttings all over the place on the walls and everywhere.

"So, you were busy following this story?" "It just doesn't add up. There is something they are covering up and they are not taking any chances either. That can put you at risk."

"What do you mean? Just for seeking the truth? He is my brother we are talking about."

"My friend died a few weeks ago."

"Did they kill him?"

"Car accident my ass. I know it was them. I just can't prove it."

"It doesn't make any sense."

"What did you find out?"

"A lot of things don't add up if you ask me." "Like what."

"The ballistic reports for instance. It showed that the senator was shot several times and that the bullets might have all come from the same gun."

"So, what's strange about it?"

"The angles in which he was shot. Look at this."

Max took out a picture and gave it to Clara. "He must have been shot from all angles. Look at the trajectory of the bullets."

"I think the government, the President got the senator shot."

"Why would he do that?"

"He was in his way if you ask me. Objecting to the new health bill I guess."

"Was he objecting?"

"No one knows. That's the only plausible explanation otherwise it doesn't make any sense."

"What's with this health bill?"

"They are trying to make it compulsory to enroll in the government protection health bill. In which the government becomes the sole health protector of everyone whether you like it or not."

"It seems that is the case even now."

Max sipped his tea and sat down.

"There is more you don't know about this bill. The government has invested all its money in making small medical devices that I quote would protect us all."

"What's wrong with that?"

"It's like surrendering yourself, your right, I mean everything and become the property of the government. I think they are using this medical device to rob banks, and innocent people and kill people at will. Speaking of gross abuse. Who knows what they have in mind. Just imagine the government using these medical devices to blind all the people in the world or mouse-trapping them blind as they call it? Speaking of modern-day slavery. You can't just invest $billions without expecting more out?"

"That's a huge motive."

Clara sat down and breathed heavily.

"Any witnesses on the day of the shooting?"

"None as far as I know."

"Anyone interviewed the senator's bodyguards?"

"Out of question considered a matter of national security."

"But you know who was there that day?" Max got up and took a small pocket diary from the table.

"Relative of the deceased. That could open some doors. Get your coat to let's go."

A woman wearing a white smock coat and reading glasses walked the long narrow corridor until she reached a closed door. She looked inside and saw a man sitting on the table. She opened the door and looked at the man and with her head signaled the man to follow her. The man was wearing a white vest, and an unfastened long shirt with military-style pants and shining shoes. He looked unconcerned about anything only answering to what he is asked shot and precise without showing emotions.

"So, what happened there? I heard you lost it." The man did not answer, or neither looked at the woman as they walked in the corridor.

"All tests seem okay. You just need time off for a few days at home will do the magic I will tell your commander. Okay."

The man simply nodded his head and left leaving the woman standing at the door looking at him. A car soon afterward hit the road and inside was the senator's bodyguard Justine with a well-shaved face with a military-style haircut. He looked around and saw everyone minding their business. It felt good to be human again, he thought. Protecting the senator was not an easy task. He had spent hours on his feet manning buildings and you name it. This was like a breath of fresh air. He scanned the road ahead of him before the car came to a halt at the traffic lights. He looked to the left side and saw a big billboard with the picture of the senator. Instantly he felt something, a sense of failure that he squinted his eyes and closed them. He quickly looked ahead and saw that the traffic lights were about to change and when he was about to drive forward a woman's voice from his right car window startled him.

"Help! Help! Please give us some change." Instantly he looked scared and frightened and for a while, he fixed his eyes on that woman with a slack-jawed face. The driver of the car behind him blasted his horn at the same time cursing and shouting. Justine suddenly drove away leaving the woman standing in the middle of the road. A quick glance in the rear-view mirror revealed the woman still standing in the middle of the road until she started asking the driver in the car behind some change as well. Justine pressed a button on the MP3 player in the car and listened to the song by Carolinadeivid called Angels on Earth. Will you protect me? Will you die for me? I am like an angel. Yet I can't protect myself. I should be protecting you from above Yet I am an angel on earth. Max and Clara were in the car talking to each other.

"Of all the bodyguards who were there that day only one behaved unusually. My friend tried to trace him before he died. I think he must have discovered something that they killed him."

"Is that where we are going now?"

"Yes. But nothing to be afraid of I understand he is overseas on duty."

Clara looked outside the window frightened, her heart beating very fast with fear. Max noticed that she was scared and tried to calm her down.

"So how close were you to your brother?" Clara looked at Max and then ahead before replying.

"Close. Very close. We used to talk every day until the past few weeks." Clara looked outside the car before continuing.

"I still can't believe he is gone."

Max touched her hand before he instantly placed both his hands onto the steering wheel. The car drove for a while without anyone talking. After a while, the car turned into a quiet street before coming to a halt under a big tree by the roadside. "Like I anticipated he is away. No one home."

Max opened the glove compartment and took out a wallet and quickly looked inside drawing out a screwdriver.

"What are you trying to do?"

"What do you think? No one at home. Come."

Max opened the door and got out hoping that Clara would follow him, but she remained seated.

"I came here to ask him questions not to break into his house. I am not coming. You go," Max smiled.

"Come I promise we won't be very long."

"Ah, what are you getting me into? My brother is dead. Do you know that?" Replied Clara reluctantly and slamming the car door behind her. The two walked stealthily into the yard of the house. It looked deserted with leaflets poking out from the letter hole in the door. Max tried to open the door before going to the back of the house.

"This is dangerous. We can be arrested for housebreaking. You know."

"Just follow me."

Max took out his wallet and knelt at the door holding the doorknob. He tried several times until the door finally opened. Clara looked at him and shook her head before the two disappeared inside. They looked in the kitchen and in the lounge area. Max opened the drawers and looked inside. He looked at Clara and pointed upstairs. Clara's heart tore apart for a minute or two with fear. Max sensed it and crept upstairs on his own, but Clara scared soon followed. Upstairs were three bedrooms. The first one they entered looked like a guest bedroom without anything apart from a nicely folded bed linen. The second looked like a normal bedroom but there was no one staying in there. They reached bedroom number three and Max pushed the door open. Slowly the door opened revealing a well-decorated bedroom with picture frames and shields on the dressing-table. Max walked to the dressing-table and picked up the picture frame and looked at it.

"Is that him?"

"Yes. He could be our answer. I understand he wasn't happy about something. I think that's the main reason why he was sent abroad soon after the incident."

"What are we looking for?"

"I don't know, anything that can explain character or anything we can use."

The pair started opening the drawers, but they could not find anything. Max opened the wardrobe and looked inside. He spotted a briefcase and took it out. He laid it on the bed and tried to open it, but it had a built-in locking system, so he took out his wallet again. Clara looked at him with talking eyes as if asking him what the fuck he was doing. Max struggled to open the briefcase.

"Wait here I will be back." Insisted Max before going out of the bedroom door. Clara screamed.

"No. You can't leave me here."

"I am just going to the car. I will be back. Okay?" Max ran out and Clara heard his footsteps and the opening and closing of the door before silence broke out. She had never felt this scared before. She looked at the picture on the dressing-table. The man seemed like a well-bred man raised in a house with loving parents. He looked very disciplined. There were photos when he was in junior and high school. At that moment she felt a bit relaxed nevertheless her heart kept beating very fast. The closing of the door downstairs startled her that she nearly peed herself but Max's voice after that calmed her nerves.

"I am back," she briefly smiled. A car turned into the road and suddenly stopped in the middle of the road. The driver quickly opened the glove compartment and took out a gun before parking the car meters away from the car under the big tree. The man disappeared soon after. Max entered the bedroom and started poking the lock with a screwdriver before using a hammer to try to force open the briefcase. Outside a man suddenly rolled onto the ground as he entered the yard and immediately he was on his knees looking down moving his head as if scanning the area. He pointed his gun looking down and fired two shots before getting up and entering the house. Stealthily with a pointed gun, he pushed the door waving the gun quickly left and then right. He looked upward and started inching forward stealthily up the stairs. He reached the bedroom and slowly pushed the door open.

"Help. Help. Help me."

He instantly dropped the gun and looked like he had seen a ghost. He stood there for a while, frightened, confused, and disoriented.

"Help."

"Who are you? Who sent you? What are you doing here? Who sent you?"

Justine quickly knelt and touched Max's neck before he clenched his fist with his arm touching his forehead and his eyes closed. He got up and looked at the bed for a while. Max had been shot in the head and died instantly. Justine watched as the blood spot became bigger and bigger. It felt like a dream. He just couldn't believe this was happening.

"Help."

Justine looked and knelt near Clara but did not touch her.

"What's going on. I did not shoot her. Who sent

you?"

Clara had been shot on her side and she was bleeding profusely. Justine sat on the bed and put his arms together after picking up the gun. Soon afterward the neighbors heard a huge scream followed by the sound of two bullets with the last bullet sound rocketing high into the skies.

CHAPTER SIX

A cake making van parked outside one of the hotels
in the city. The man in uniform standing outside the
hotel ran to open the doors. The two men in the van
opened the doors and pushed a trolley with a
wedding cake. Everyone looked at the cake and
smiled. The women with their husbands once they
have seen the cake, they would hug their husbands
and kiss them. The men who delivered the cake
would look at the couple and shake their heads in
appreciation. The two men arrive at the reception
where they were greeted by Gemma, whose face
looked radiant at the sight of the cake. She cast a
friendly smile and winked at the delivery men.

"This way," she shouted pointing. The cake was
well decorated with a couple on top hugging each
other and well dressed up with flowers on the side.

"Over there please," shouted Gemma. The man left

the cake where Gemma had told them to and they bowed in appreciation as everyone applauded clapping their hands. "Thank you. Thank you. It's a pleasure." The men soon disappeared.

"The cake is here everyone!" Shouted Gemma excited.

"Excellent! Bellissimo!" Shouted Franco. People gathered just to see the cake.

"I want to see the look on her face. Beautifully well-decorated cake. Love it to bits."

"I will go and tell her that the cake is here." Clarissa, Kate's best friend ran upstairs. She knocked on the door and waited.

"Just a minute. Who is it?"

"Clarissa open the door."

"It's open come on in."

She danced holding the long dress off the floor.

"I have never been this excited before. I feel like a young girl."

Clarissa looked at Kate and instantly stopped dancing and walked to her friend. "What seems to be the problem? Why are you crying? This is your best day why are you crying?" Clarissa took Kate's hand and walked with her to the bed. Kate was crying her eyes had turned red.

"I don't understand. I thought I would find you happy and smiling."

"It's nothing. I just wish my dad was here." "Oh, I see."

"I can't stop thinking about him. I know he will be very happy for me."

"Wherever he is he loves you very much." "I know I just miss him. I last saw him when I was a little girl. I can't stop thinking about the last time I saw him. I cried till my eyes turned red. He just walked away. For days I cried myself to sleep." Clarissa took out a handkerchief and gave it to Kate.

"What happened the last time you saw him."

"Something was wrong. I think someone was blackmailing him. He changed after a few weeks. He was the best dad anyone can wish for. He used to spend time with me. He used to call me his princess. One night I woke up in the middle of the night." Clarissa waited as Kate wiped the tears on her cheeks.

"I couldn't sleep so I went to talk to mum. Mum was fast asleep, and dad was sat there on the bed crying. He kissed me on the forehead and on the cheeks. He said I love you very much, but I have to go to work."

"Very sorry to hear that. So, is that the last time you saw him?"

"The next morning mom woke me up. Dad was on the floor shivering and shaking." "Was he sick?"

"I guess but mum said he was taking drugs. You know like rock stars."

"Drugs? Hard to believe."

"He said it was to ease the pain after the accident."

"That makes sense."

"After the hospital operation, he changed. He was in pain all the time. He once told me that the doctors were torturing him?" "Doctors?"

"You don't believe me?"

"It's not that it's just hard to believe that people who made an oath to help and heal would actually cause such misery." "Doctors are evil maybe not all of them but they tortured him until he started taking drugs to ease the pain and not the other way around. Why would he lie about doctors? He was the best dad you can have. He changed only after the hospital operation. Mum said he told her that he was going away to protect me and mum." "They might have tortured him." A man came out of the house and jumped on his motorbike. He was about to put on his helmet when a little girl maybe 4 years old came out of the house.

"Daddy, daddy. Can I go with you?" the man smiled.

"Of course, my princess."

He lifted the girl and kissed her on the head and placed her on the motorbike. "Where do you want to go?"

"I don't know. Maybe town and buy me a princess doll." The door suddenly opened. "Kate stay with me. Keep me company. Come. Let daddy go."

"But mommy I want to go because daddy is going to buy me a princess doll."

"Your father is going to work."

"But mum he said he will go with me." "Come let your daddy go."

"But mum."

"Bye, my princess see you soon. I will bring the princess doll for you."

"OK, daddy I will stay with mum."

The man wore his helmet and started the motorbike

before he disappeared. Miles away the man was driving on the road thinking about his wife and his daughter when he suddenly saw a man knelt in the middle of the road. It was after a bend that he tried to avoid hitting the man when he lost control of the motorbike falling onto the road before the motorbike crashed his leg as it landed on him. Whilst down he raised his head to look if the man was okay, but the man had disappeared and never even tried to help. A passerby spotted him that's when he was taken to the hospital. The leg was broken, and the doctors suggested that he needed a metal plate, or he risked losing his leg. He had no option, so he agreed. Months after that's when his nightmares began. The doctors started torturing him. They had implanted a small drone-like-medical device in his leg which they remotely operated. At least that is what the leaked X-rays showed. The girl waited outside hoping that her dad would bring her a doll of a princess, but he didn't return that day. She cried and cried until she can't cry. Clarissa stood up and touched Kate's hand before pulling her up.

"Come and see the cake. It's beautiful you will love it."

"I just wish he was here you know?"

Kate and Clarissa rushed downstairs. Kate was very happy to see the cake exactly like she wanted it to be. On the table was an enveloped card addressed to her. She looked at Clarissa before taking the card to

read it. 'Chic, chic, chic, mwah, mwah, mwah.'
Kate quickly looked around with an excited face.
She ran outside to look around. She saw a man
walking away on the pavement. When she saw his
back view, she ran after him very fast holding the
wedding dress high up.

"Daddy! Daddy! Daddy!"

She ran as if her legs were going to break. She had a
flashback of the day her daddy left after promising
her to bring a princess-doll for her. Somehow it felt
like that day if he had returned that's how she might
have felt. She cried tears of joy as she ran after the
man. She caught up with the man and instinctively
hugged him.

"Daddy! Daddy!"

The man turned around and looked at her. She
looked at the man and sobbed uncontrollably.

"Wish you the best on your wedding day. Good
luck."

The man turned around and left. Soon afterward
Clarissa arrived breathing very hard and hugged
her.

"I just wish he was here you know."

The two women sobbed profusely hugging each
other. A man parked his car and got out limping. An

SUV arrived soon after and parked next to the man's vehicle. " Have you made that claim yet? We want our money."

"Leave me alone I have suffered enough already. Can you find someone else to nag?"

"Oh, maybe your daughter."

"Bastards you touch her, and I will kill you. Don't even think about it."

"Our money or..."

The man was pushed to the ground and stamped on the injured leg before the pain from his leg nearly shut down his system. The men jumped into the SUV and left. "Do you think he will make the claim?"

"He has to, or we get nothing."

"Do you think he will get anything?"

The man laughed uncontrollably.

"Are you stupid? If he gets something, then we don't get anything."

"I don't understand. If he gets something, then we can ask for our money isn't that right?"

The man mockingly laughed again.

"You, dumb ass. He must make a claim then we step in. The doctors will do their bit and then we come in. We discredit him and ask a percentage of what he is asking from the insurance company. We get the money without paying any taxes all at once. Get it dopey. In other words, he works for us. Get it?"

"Help me out here let me get this straight. You broke his leg. So that he can make a claim, right? So that we come in and discredit him so that he won't get anything, but we get something by supplying information to the insurance company. What kind of information.?" "Can't you see that he is a drug user. Maybe hooked on heroin. Can't you see that?" "No, he seems alright. If you were not in the middle of the road, he could not have crashed."

"Do you want me to smack you? I said that he is a heroin user. He had an accident. Fault of his own."

"But you were in the middle of the road." "He was hallucinating. Who on earth would do that? Who will believe that? If you ask him right now, he will tell you that after the accident he did not see the man in the road."

"Because you ran away, you, spineless monster."

"Sure, I am going to smack you. He did not see the man after the accident because the pain made him sober. All the drugs. Gone! I told you drugs are very bad."

"Tests will prove otherwise."

"That's when the doctor comes in. He is going to torture him until he starts taking drugs. He is going to lose everything. Wife, job, car and even his daughter. That brings someone else of value to work for us." "Who?"

"His daughter."

"She is only maybe 5 or 6 what can she do for us?"

"Get us another softy we can cream and dispose of. The possibilities are endless!"
"How do you sleep at night?"

"Now you see why I don't want kids of my own. On my own, I can live up to 100 years. Have a kid. These evil monsters will start grooming the whole family until you are dead. After that, they take your kids too. They are never satisfied. They will never stop at anything. When they say they want to help you say help your son or your daughter first. Greedy evil bastards."

"So why you work for them then?"

"Hey, don't try to be a smart ass with me. The President himself works for them. If the world if so fucked up what can I do? I have bills to pay you know?"

"After this, I am out."

"Just wait tomorrow the doctor is going to make that man commit suicide."

"Are doctors not supposed to have morals?" "In fairy-tales only. This is a big business, a big money-spinner. Who cares about morals anymore?"

"If this was your daughter, I just wonder how you would react."

"I will never have children of my own. Full stop."

The following day the injured man spent the full day with his daughter and wife. At night his phone rang, and he spoke on the phone. He entered his bedroom and took out his folder and looked inside. He took out some papers and signed them and after that, he went outside and posted the letters in the letterbox. He came back and slept. He was woken up by a phone call and he went into the bathroom and spoke.

"Leave my daughter out of this. I sent the letters canceling the claim. Just promise me that you won't touch my daughter. No matter what. You will never separate her from her mother. Don't try again to make them fight. I signed the will. I will leave tonight after the phone call. But if it wasn't for the safety of my daughter, I would kill you myself."

The man slumped down and cried before he felt the most excruciating pain. He lay on the bathroom floor and cried. The pain was unbearable. His wife and child woke up after hearing his cries.

"Daddy, what is wrong? Why are you crying? Daddy stop crying!"

The little girl started crying before the man got up.

"My leg again. I must go and see the doctor. Okay. Bye, my love and bye my princess."

The man kissed his wife and looked at her for a long time with tears coming from his eyes. He kissed the girl on the forehead and the cheeks.

"Look after mummy for me until I get back okay?"

"Okay, daddy. Come back soon promise." The man just looked and wiped the tears on his cheeks before closing the door behind him.

CHAPTER SEVEN

A cat ran from the parking area across the road
through an opening in the fence and crossed the
main road. A car suddenly passed by narrowly
missing the cat. It meowed loudly as the car tires
nearly ran-over its tail. It stopped and sat down. It
lifted one of its back legs and licked its tail before
proceeding toward a huge house. It entered the
house through the small hole in the door and
quickly ran upstairs meowing. The bedroom door
was open, and the cat entered inside and jumped
onto the bed. A lady was on top of a man on the bed
both kissing with both their hands in each other's
arms, clasped together. The woman raised her upper
body, and instantly the cat jumped down onto the
carpet. The woman wriggled her waist on top of the
man. That went on for a while before the cat heard
the orgasmic screams from the woman and the
growling noises made by the man. Quickly the cat
ran downstairs and licked the empty food bowl. A

naked woman soon followed downstairs and opened the refrigerator. The cat meowed brushing itself against the woman's leg. The woman opened the cupboard and took out the cat's food and knelt and filled the food bowl. Immediately after the woman went upstairs butt naked.

"So, when are you planning to come back?" "As soon as the conference is over."

The woman sat on the bed and quickly jumped on top of the man. She kissed him everywhere his chest, his stomach, his lips before she started rubbing her body against his. She quickly put her hand between her legs lying on top of the man before lifting her buttocks up and instantly slumped down on top of the man. The man groaned. Downstairs the cat stopped eating the food as the noises from upstairs became louder and louder. A loud scream from the bedroom frightened the cat that it jumped out of the house through the small opening in the door. It stopped while outside and heard the woman laughing upstairs. It looked up and soon disappeared. Jayden hugged Katrine as she lay on top of him. She raised her head and looked at him. She gazed into his eyes for a few seconds before she smiled and touched his lips and instantly planted some kisses on his lips.

"We can do this all day you know but I have to go Jay. You know that."

"Just want to be close to you."

"I will just be gone for a few days."

"Seems like a long time without your smile."

"So sweet."

"Promise I will be back before you know it."

"I can't get enough of you."

"OK come on top."

Jayden rolled to the side before getting up. Immediately he passionately kissed every soft part on Katrine's body before he pressed down her thighs against the bed. She lifted her head and looked as he moved his tongue all over her body. She sighed passionately before tilting her head backward and started moaning passionately. Later that day Katrine got out of the house and strolled out of the gate to a waiting taxi outside. She opened the door and was about to get in when Jayden came out of the house wearing a white robe. "Jayden, I have to go you know that." Jayden walked to the taxi and kissed her. The two were in each other's arms for a while. The taxi driver cleared his throat. Katrine stopped kissing Jayden and smiled. "I have to go darling. See you soon." Jayden stepped backward and looked on as Katrine got into the taxi before the taxi disappeared around the corner. The cat meowed and came running to Jayden who in turn knelt and rubbed its head before carrying it into the house. The airport was busy as usual with people coming in and out of the airport. The taxi arrived, and Katrine got out of the taxi and waited for the taxi driver to take out her traveling bag. Quickly she dragged the bad on its wheels into the airport. She looked at the huge display screen and headed upstairs. Up the stairs before she joined a long queue that quickly disappeared once the doors were opened. She handed her passport and looked around. "Thank you. Enjoy your flight." "I will." Replied Katrine taking back her passport. She walked toward the boarding door. A man was seated in the waiting area and for a second or two, she stopped walking and looked at the man. She smiled and thought about Jayden. She had finally found happiness in Jayden. Soon after she found herself at the plane door. The air hostess welcomed her in and looked at her boarding pass and said something that fell on deaf ears. Katrine was thinking about the sex session that morning with Jayden. That left her feeling like a teenager in heat. She pressed her legs hard as she sat down. She took out her phone and rang Jayden. The phone rang, but no one answered the call. "Ladies and gentlemen, I am your captain. Soon the plane will be ready for takeoff. Please fasten your seat belts."

The air hostess soon stood in front of everyone giving instructions. Katrine after traveling many times now she had heard that message many times that she simply looked outside the window. Soon after the flight took off. The control tower was busy as usual. Everyone looked at the small screens in front of them with headphones on their heads speaking into them. A man walked into the tower with a coffee cup in his hand. He looked at the big screen and drank his coffee. He soon left the tower down the elevators. A motorcade of black SUVs and limousines made its way to the buildings in the city. The front SUV sped ahead flashing blue lights. The two limousines entered the building following the security services cars ahead and being followed by other SUVs with security services. The President got out and was whizzed into the building. A man came running toward him.

"We have a problem."

"Yes."

"Come this way, Mr. President."

The President and the secret servicemen followed the man into a huge room.

"We just heard calls from the tower I mean from all towers after an influx of mayday calls."

The man stopped talking and took off his glasses. He looked at the President and everyone.

"What seemed to be the problem?" asked the President. Isabella ran into the house and answered the call.

"Hello."

"Listen very careful darling something happened to me I mean to us."

"What do you mean?"

"The captain has just announced that we have to agree..."

"Agree to what?"

"Call the authorities."

"And say what?"

Soon the line went dead. Isabella frantically dialed the emergency numbers. "Hello, what seems to be the problem?"

"I think my husband is in trouble."

"Where is your husband Ma'am?"

"He is on a plane... Flight eh... 512,"

"In a plane has the plane been hijacked?" "Not sure but it seems the captain is demanding my husband to agree to something."

"Are you sure? Did he say he is in danger?" In the plane, Scarlett dialed a number and listened impatiently.

"Come on pick up the phone. Pick up." Soon the voice mail message came up. "Listen Declan. Something happened to me. To us. I am on the plane. It seems the captain is blackmailing us. For some reason, I can't see. Please call the authorities."

In the tower, the staff in the tower received numerous mayday calls.

"Mayday. Mayday! We need help. We are flying on autopilot and seems to go nowhere. Our fuel is running out."

"Can you land? Find the nearest airport and land."

Soon after the line went dead.

"Did he get the message?"

The other tower member of staff asked. "It's just not one plane. Look it seems all the planes are in distress."

"Why can't they just land at the nearest airport?"

In the building in the city center, the President stood up and walked to the window. He looked outside. He walked back to the center of the room.

"Is it a plane hijack?"

"No. But we have intercepted a message. Listen to this."

The man reached for a tape recorder on the desk and played a message.

"I am your new guardian angel. Only I can decide when you shall live, or you shall die. As you all know. You can see that I have taken control of everyone. We can come to an agreement. From today you shall surrender yourself to me in exchange for your being especially your sight. To those who want back their life, you shall sign papers agreeing that you belong to me and you shall be the property of the New Driver..."

The President sat down, and everyone looked speechless.

"Can they still land?"

"If they can't see, how are they going to input the landing coordinates?"

"What are their options?"

"Fly around on autopilot."

"And then."

No one answered, but all just looked with sad faces that seemed to say, death.

"Send fighter jets."

Shouted the President.

"Mr. President, we don't know what we are dealing with. I think it's better first to get more information before sending more planes out there. It's not our country only it's the whole world. Look.

" The man switched on the big screen that showed a lot of planes hovering in circles in the air without landing.

"Oh my God. Who on earth would do something like this?"

"He calls himself the New Driver."

"What does he want?"

"Nothing. He wants everyone to be his property."

"So, killing all these people will achieve that?"

"Fear. Fear, Mr. President."

"What time do we have here?"

"Max four hours of fuel reserves."

"I can't just sit here and watch."

Quickly the President got into his limousine and the Presidential motorcade sped off. In the tower, everyone gathered around looking at the big screen lined with flashing dots.

"Can they use autopilot to land?"

"Clear the way! Clear the way! Coming through. The President." The President and his security servicemen entered the tower.

"It's global. Somehow he has taken hold of the universe."

"Global how is that possible?"

"We don't know but it's not looking good." "What does he want?"

"It seems he is talking through the captain."

The President looked at the senior member of staff and he nodded.

"Flight 512. Are you receiving this is the tower?" There was no answer. Everyone looked at the President.

"Flight 512. It's the tower. Are you receiving?"

"Go ahead. Receiving loud and clear." "What's your status."

"Flying on autopilot."

"Can you land?"

"I understand on this plane it's possible since it's a new plane but has never been put into practice."

"What seems to be the main problem." "Somehow our system has been hijacked and we are all blinded."

"How much fuel is left?"

"Two hours at most."

"We have emergency calls from your passenger that you the captain is blackmailing passengers."

"Not all what it seems. Just passing the message."

"Who is behind this?"

"New Driver. The new driver as he calls himself."

"New driver?"

"Try to land on autopilot."

"I don't think it's a clever idea."

"Captain what other options do you have?" "Everyone cooperates, and everything will be okay?"

"You mean wait until it's too late?"

"Goddammit land that plane captain. This is the President speaking."

Silence broke out. Everyone looked at the President and listened to what the captain was going to say.

"Copy that Mr. President," replied the captain calmly. Everyone looked at the big screen and listened. The captain frantically searched for the autopilot and looked for the buttons. He stopped and visualized the buttons. He stopped and concentrated for a while. He visualized the cockpit and all the buttons. Instinctively he pressed the buttons before an automated voice startled everyone.

"Autopilot landing activated please confirm now."

The Captain frantically searched for the enter button. He stopped and visualized the cockpit again before reaching for a button and pressed it.

"Auto-land activated."

The plane flew for a few minutes going down. Women and children cried holding the seats as the altitude of the plane altered as it descended. People cried some praying to God.

"Do you know what altitude we are on?" asked the co-pilot.

"How can I know? Do you know?"

"No that's why I have asked you."

"Between 25 to 20m above ground?" "Should it not be 15m above ground?" "Listen. Ask the tower. They know?"

"They just want the plane landing."

"You are going to kill us all."

"When it's 15m above the ground, the radar altimeter will correct itself and choose the correct landing path. I read this somewhere."

Instantly the plane shook, and a constant beeping sound was heard followed by another automated voice.

"Turbulence conditions please fasten your seat belts."

"Nothing to worry about we are just a few meters above the safe auto-land height of 15m above ground level."

The plane shock in turbulence waves. The oxygen masks fell in front of the passengers. Everyone men, women and children cried as the plane nose-dived.

"22 meters above ground level. Auto-land quickly engaged." The plane shook as it nose-dived. A consistent beeping noise startled the passengers.

The luggage cabinets above seats opened, and the luggage fell in front of passengers. People screamed and cried. Some wore oxygen masks that had dropped whilst others hung on to their seats. The plane shook in the turbulence waves before an emergency beeping sound is released. The plane was losing altitude very fast than it normally would. A constant beeping sound is heard on the plane.

"When we reach the 15m height above ground level auto-land will automatically take over and correct the problem," said the Captain. The beeping sound and the shaking continued for some time before an automated message is announced.

"Auto-land disengaged. 12m above ground." The Captain looked in the direction the co-pilot was. He quickly searched for the cockpit buttons and looked for the auto-land button.

"10 meters above ground."

The turbulence proceeded on with the plane shaking and the plane nose-diving that the passengers were thrown in front of the plane.

"6 meters above ground."

The captain looked in the direction the co-pilot's voice was coming from. He tried to activate the auto-land, but the turbulence was so enormous that activating the auto-land was impossible. The President looked on the big screen like everyone else. The plane was losing altitude very fast than what seemed to be normal.

"Is that normal?" asked the President. "Flight 512. Do you copy?"

"This is flight 512. Loud and clear."

"You are losing altitude very fast."

"Auto-land malfunctioned."

Everyone looked at each other and then at the President. The plane nosedived at a steep angle before the screen turned red and a flashing message emerged on the screen.

"Impact. Crash."

"Oh my God!"

Shouted one of the men in the tower. Soon after that planes started falling to the ground either because they have run out of jet fuel or because the pilots tried to land without their eyesight or that auto-land malfunctioned. The President and everyone else looked on, unable to do anything. The world looked on televisions as the reports of accidents all over the world were announced that all planes in the air that day were doomed. Fear, the greatest fear ever felt by mankind spread like wildfires. People just sat around televisions and watch the news as the stories unfolded. All the leaders of the world felt powerless and helpless. A new and equally challenging emerging power was on the horizon. The New Driver had sent out a clear message. Obey or perish. Do or die. Everyone was now the property of this New Driver or die instantly a horrendous death. The New Driver as he called himself meant business. Planes all over the world had crashed to the ground with or without auto-land. The people first frantically panicked when they lost their sight only to be killed that way. Everyone asked who on earth would be so heartless and evil? The passengers had sent last phone calls to their loved ones explaining what they have been subjected to. The President feeling powerless and traumatized succumbed unable to think or find a solution. The New Driver was there to stay. The next day it was all public transport. Cars running into each other on the roads at junctions and everywhere. Numerous head-on coalitions reported in several countries. People stopping cars in the middle-of-the-road and getting out were reports that dominated the morning papers. Trains shooting past the stopping stations and later colliding with each other. Globally everyone stopped going to work. The fear of dying was so real that three-quarters of the world population stayed at home indoors at home in case they fall victim to this New Driver. Everyone sat next to the television sets. In every home, the whole family sat close to the television sets watching the news fearing to lose their sight first after being mousetrapped-blind by the New Driver. The reporters would document all cases all day and night. The medical bill was made compulsory a few years back worldwide. This was only the tip of the iceberg. People started realizing what they had signed themselves to. Collisions, plane crashes, trains colliding with each other, people being hit by cars as they stood in the middle-of-the-road you name it. Fear spread like bush fires. The New Driver brought the entire world to a standstill. In the capital a man looked agitated before running to a coffee shop. He ordered coffee before sitting down. He looked around quickly scanning the area. He only sipped his coffee for a bit and quickly left the coffee shop. He was wearing reading glasses and had a suit and was carrying a newspaper which he frequently used to cover his face. He stopped outside one of the buildings in the city and looked around. He blew his nose and rubbed his fingers on his coat. He pushed the heavy door and entered the building. He entered the building and quickly opened his jacket. He looked down and quickly closed the jacket as soon as another person entered the elevator. He looked like someone on drugs or someone who has been running. He breathed heavily and looked very agitated. He waited outside a building and pressed a button. A man answered on the PA system.

"How can we help you?"

"I have an appointment with the head of Communications."

"Your name?"

"Alfred Jones,"

"OK come in."

As soon as Alfred entered the corporation building, he pulled his gun and pointed at everyone waiving his gun as he entered the broadcasting studios. A woman was on-air reading the news bulletin. Alfred pointed a gun at her whilst placing a hand over his lips. He moved in close to the woman who remained seated. Alfred shook his head before pointing the gun on her forehead. She quickly stood up before Alfred placed the barrel of the gun between her buttocks moving the barrel up and down before poking the woman between the legs with the gun. The woman quickly jumped away. Alfred put the gun on his waist belt before sitting down. He sat down and looked in front and saw lines coming down one of the screens in front of him. He read the message as the lines went down before they disappeared. He looked at the screen in front of him. "I am the New Driver. From today until further notice you all belong to the New Driver Ltd. You are all the property of the New Driver Ltd. You have to say it loud that you belonged to the New Driver Ltd. You are all property of New Driver Ltd. I repeat. Failure to pledge allegiance will result in one thing. Death or loss of your sight permanently. I am sure by now you know what I can and can't do. First, I can kill all of you in cold blood. Secondly, I will not tolerate any disobedience. Any revolts will only witness more deaths." After the speech, Alfred struggled to read any more from the message he had prepared. He tried to get up but staggered everywhere before he pulled his gun and started talking to himself.

"You said that you will let me go after this..."

He looked around and listened.

"You are a lying bastard. You know what? Do this yourself you bastard."

The man placed the gun in his mouth. The woman screamed. The man took off the gun from his mouth and looked at the woman before smiling. Suddenly he placed the gun again into his mouth and pulled the trigger on national television. Worldwide trains, planes, cars you name it everything was involved in accidents, head-on collision and all kinds of accidents. People were very afraid to leave their houses after that. A car pulled up outside a government building in the city center. A man came out leaving the car door open. He staggered outside and cursed.

"Where is this New Driver?"

"Sir stay away from the gate. Unless you have an appointment, please move away from the gates. You will be shot dead if you don't move away," said the security serviceman at the gate.

"Where is this New Driver? I will never sign anything. I will never give away my freedom. I am not anyone's property. I refuse with all the hairs on my head to be someone's property. I will fight until the end."

"Move away from the gate or you will be shot," shouted the security officer pointing a gun at the man.

"Whose side are you on?"

"I don't care. Move away from the gate."

"I want to see this New Driver. I want to kill this bastard. Where is he? I will never lose my freedom. He can take away my sight. He can fry me. He can break all my limbs, but I will never be someone's property. I am a human being with rights. I am not a property. I will kill this bastard. Tell me where he is right now. You can scare the universe, not me." The man fired shots in the air.

"Hold it. Throw your gun down now or else I will shoot you. Get on the ground now."

The man looked shocked and surprised. "Don't take it on me. I am looking for this New Driver too."

"Get down! Get down! Throw away your weapon now. Hand's on your head now." The man refused and started walking away from the building.

"I am on your side. I want this New Driver. I can never be someone's property. I would rather die."

Another security man came running from behind the building when he heard the commotion. He just took one look and opened fire at the man."

"What are you doing? I had everything under control."

"He is holding a gun. Every reason to blow his head off."

"Jesus! He is looking for a New Driver. You didn't have to shoot him."

"It might have been you. Don't take chances."

For the coming weeks, no one left their houses or went to work. No planes flew from the airports. No trains traveled, and no buses traveled. The world stood still. Everyone was scared to go out in case they are caught in the trap. Everyone men, women, children and the old all talked about the New Driver until a time when that name seemed sacred. After that, no one wanted to mention that name again. Anyone who mentioned that name ended up losing their sight as the New Driver considered mentioning his name as a direct acceptance of allegiances. The Presidential motorcade made its way to the Presidential building in the city center. The motorcade arrived before the limousine parked outside the building. The President got out and entered the building.

"What do we know about this New Driver?"

"Ruthless. Means business."

"I want to know what he wants. Where he lives and how we can get a hold of him. I want him dead. I am the President, not someone's property. Find him!" Shouted the President. Cyrus whispered into Dalton's ears.

"What is it, Cyrus? You can talk to me." "Mr. President."

Cyrus leaned and whispered something into the President's ears.

"What are we waiting for? Let's go."

"But Mr. President."

"I will never be someone's property. If that means fighting to death so be it. Let's go." Commanded the President. The leading SUV flashed its lights clearing the way for the Presidential motorcade. The President's motorcade arrived outside the bank in the city. Quickly the security services broke into the bank and quickly the men advanced upstairs into the Managing Director of Investment's office. They broke in. When the security services were sure that the place was clear the President was led in. He entered the office and looked around. He sat on the desk and picked up the picture frame on the desk. He looked at the picture.

"How is she connected?"

"We have reason to believe that she encountered this New Driver. A phone call was traced back to this office."

"Did she ask for help?"

"Yes. She only said something happened to her and hung up. She sounded very traumatized."

"Do we know where she lives? Who is the man in the picture with her?"

"We are getting that information as we speak. The man seems to be her boyfriend."

The Presidential motorcade of six SUVs carrying the security services and two limousines carrying the President with one of them being a decoy left the bank in the city and headed toward the suburb area. A brand new red BMW X6 SUV was parked outside a mansion in the suburbs. Inside was Vicky and Mart on the bed making love.

"Don't move."

She yelled lifting her buttocks off the bed with her legs wrapped around Mart's waist. She squeezed her breast before moisturizing her fingertips and started rubbing her nipples.

"Hold my buttocks lift them high. Don't move."

Whispered Vicky stroking her clitoris opening it and closing it quickly tilting her head sideways and lifting her head before lowering it. Lowering her head as she closed the clitoral hood and lifting her head up as she fully opened the clitoral hood. That went on for some time before she intensified the rubbing and squeezing of her tits. Mart got carried away and instinctively started humping her thrusting as hard as he can.

"I said don't move."

Mart squeezed her tits very hard as she played with her clitoral hood. Moments later blood started covering her face. The more she felt excited the more blood rushed to her face, her nipple area and the area surrounding the hood.

"Oh my God."

Yelled Mart as she started drooling.

"What are you waiting for?"

Mart felt a sudden rush of blood down his waist. He felt rubbing against Vicky's inner soft parts. He looked at her and gradually pressed hard. Harder and harder with every move until Vicky was all red. Mart squeezed Vicky's buttocks and licked her nipples. She briefly looked at him before she closed her eyes and grabbed Mart very tight. She pulled him against herself until she felt an intense feeling that she squirted so hard and had multiple orgasms one after the other lasting just a few seconds in between. Mart looked on as Vicky was still rubbing her clitoris having small short orgasms. He smiled. He had never experienced anything like that before. When she had the last short orgasm, she giggled and slumped onto the bed and fell asleep for a while. Mart looked at her while she slept nude. He kissed her on the stomach going up. She smiled and looked at him.

"Too late now. I must sleep. I climaxed too many times."

"It's such a turn on watching you have multiple orgasms. I didn't know I was that good. My ex-girlfriend never had an orgasm like that. I climax more than I normally do."

Vicky got up and sat on the bed.

"Really?"

"Cross my heart."

"I knew it. It could be that thing between my legs. I just don't know how to remove it." Mart quickly sat on the bed.

"What? Why want to get rid of something that gives you such joy."

"Just for a short while after that, I feel used, vulnerable and abused just imagine someone else playing with your private parts."

"Excuse me. I should be the one saying that. All the way it's you in charge. Stop! Don't Move. Squeeze my tits. So how can you say that? Me abusing you? I don't think so."

"There is something between my legs making me very horny."

"Everyone knows that. I can see that thing right now."

Mart leaned down to look at Vicky's shining vagina puffing out his cum every time she breathed.

"Beautiful. I think I can look at it forever." Mart kissed her stomach and slowly inched toward her vagina. He licked her clitoral hood and held the clitoris between his soft lips and pulled it up.

"Mart, you don't understand."

"I still find it hard to believe that you would want to remove a God-given gift for giving you such pleasure."

"Sit down there is something I want to tell you."

Vicky grabbed the pillow and covered the area between her legs.

"I am sorry Mart. I was weak and vulnerable. I think all this is a mistake. After David left me. I didn't know what to do. I was craving for someone. That thing between my legs wouldn't stop. Just couldn't stop. There you were gagging for it."

"Whoa. I am an adult. I gave full consent. In fact, I love sex. I mean the lovemaking."

Vicky sighed heavily and looked at Mart. "What about the risks?"

"What risks?"

Mart looked at Vicky and laughed.

"A very good one."

"I am not joking. Just imagine someone is helping you orgasm like a teenager. What do they want? What's in for them. Honestly, I should not have got you involved. I think you should leave and never come back."

"What are you talking about?"

"Go! Go! Go! Go!"

Shouted a strong man's voice. The front door to the mansion was kicked open. Vicky screamed and hugged Mart before covering both with bed linen.

"Vicky?"

"Yes. Mr. President. What are you doing here?"

"I understand you have information for me. Who did it? I saw a brand-new car outside. Let me see that's over $69 000. Is this David?"

"I didn't do it. No this is not David."

The President looked at Mart and walked next to him.

"Are you using this young man too? Do you work in the bank?"

"Vicky, what is this about?"

Mart looked at Vicky surprised and shocked. The security man approached Mart and held his neck.

"Answer the President's question."

"Yes, I work in the bank, but I am not David."

"The security man quickly put the gun onto Mart's head. Vicky hysterically screamed.

"He is not involved! Don't kill him. I dragged him into this. Please let him go. I will tell you everything you want to know. He is innocent."

The President took out the robe and walked toward

Vicky. He covered her and sighed.

"We traced back a phone call to your office."

"What phone call?"

"The call you made after stealing $1 billion from the bank."

The President smiled. Vicky looked at the President and looked down.

"Who told you that?"

"FBI. My boys are good you know."

Vicky walked away from the President. She looked outside the window and saw her brand-new Land-rover outside. Her heart split into two. She started putting everything together.

"Clever bastard." She cursed.

"Sorry. You say?" asked the President inching forward closer to Vicky.

"This young gentleman helped you in exchange for sex?"

"I did not Mr. President. He is not involved."

"Don't worry I am not bothered about the money. I am not the CEO of the bank."

The President smiled and looked at Vicky. "I want the man who did this. This clever manipulating son of a bitch. I can't wait to have my hands around his neck and choke him to death until his eyes popped out." The President said this choking Vicky. "Mr. President! Mr. President. She is a victim caught up in all this."

The President stopped and looked at the security serviceman and at Vicky who instantly slumped to the ground choking. "You said she got the money. So, she knows this New Driver. How did she get all that money in such a brief time?"

"The New Driver is very clever he must have set her up."

"But she won't talk to me. I am the President. I can't be lied to too."

The security serviceman moved in on Mart. He had witnessed all this. Vicky shouted and screamed.

"Please let him go. He is innocent. I will tell you everything."

"Does anyone understand and respect the President around here? What must I do to be feared and respected? I am the one in power and control. Not this calculating manipulating bastard. Get answers or waste both. We have enough evidence to put this behind us. I must be feared. I am saddened when people lie to me in front of my men. What a picture does this reflect?" The President was shaking with anger, rage and a sense of fear detected in his voice patterns. The New Driver had instilled and implanted fear worldwide and clearly, the President was not immune. He showed signs of fear of being shaken with every day the New Driver was at large. The President walked out of the mansion and into the limousine outside. The other men followed leaving only two men with Vicky and Mart. When the President's motorcade had disappeared, the serviceman unfastened Vicky's robe and looked at her naked body. She quickly looked down and got hold of the ends of robe's fastening ropes and before she had the chance to cover her nude body, the man had his hands on her neck. In the other room, Mart was punched at the back of the head and fell. The man took out a silencer and picked up a sofa cushion. He took a long breath and knelt as Mart lay naked and unconscious. He placed a pillow on Mart's head and pointed the extended gun barrel. He folded his mouth and pulled the trigger. He waited for his mate. He heard the struggle in the bedroom and walked to the bedroom door. The man was on top of Vicky choking her to death. Her legs were on his stomach pushing him very hard fighting for her life. Soon her eyes started turning red as she choked.

"Hurry up. Let's go. You should have finished her by now."

The other man did not reply. The man standing at

the door took out his gun and refastened the silencer he had already removed from his gun and looked around. Instantly he threw himself to the ground and rolled on his side before getting up on his knees with his eyes closed and scanned the whole area.

"Vicky let out a loud scream at the same time squirting so hard that something jumped from her into the man that he screamed as well before slumping to the ground next to her. The other security serviceman who was on his knees scanning the area got frightened by all these screams that he opened his eyes to find his mate down and Vicky laying down next to him lifeless.

"What happened?"

"I can't see. Get me out of here."

"I think we have company."

"I know. I sensed someone too outside." "Check if she is dead. If not finish her off." "Give me your gun."

"No, you can't use a gun. Choke her to death."

"What?"

"Like what the President said."

"I don't have time for this."

Said the man checking the gun.

"The jealous boyfriend returned home and found his girlfriend screwing another man in their bed. He picked up the gun and shot the lover. He then strangled his girlfriend to death and then ran away. Manhunt." "Where is this boyfriend?"

"Dead weeks ago."

"So, who is outside?"

Stanley checked his backup gun and briefly looked outside.

"Wait here I will go and investigate."

"No. Don't leave me here like this. Take me to the car I can help you scan. I am not blind."

Kai had a point. Stanley helped lift Kai up and walked him out of the building. Outside the mansion, Kai leaned against the walls as Stanley suddenly rolled to the ground before kneeling on the ground looking down scanning the area. The two men instinctively fired shots in the bushes surrounding the mansion.

"Just get me out of here before we get ambushed. After all, neighbors might see us."

"You got a point. Let's go."

The black SUV disappeared in the dark with the lights switched off.

CHAPTER EIGHT

Years Ago.

A man ran in a park and a dog chased after him but when it was in his reach the dog turned around and ran back the way it came. The man threw himself to the ground and rolled on the ground breathing heavily. He laughed and raised his head looking where the dog went. It soon made sense why the dog ran back. A small boy was on and off the ground struggling to run and breathe at the same time. The dog quickly brushed against the boy leaving him slumped on the floor. "Come on! You can do it."

Shouted the man as the boy laughed and fell to the ground. As soon as he got up, the dog came and knocked him to the ground and ran to Adam. Adam looked and cheered on. The boy laughed and got up and ran toward his daddy. By this time, he was close, yet the dog came and knocked him down before it sped off to Adam. "Oscar. No playing dirty. Don't knock the boy down."

The dog feeling jealous jumped up and down and rubbed itself on Adam. Adam sensed it and picked up the dog. He rubbed the dog's fur. He hugged the dog and held the dog in his arms. The boy looked and frowned. He got up and looked at his daddy holding the dog in his hand. He stood there and scanned the whole area. He looked at the distance he must cover before he reached his dad. The more he looked at his daddy hugging the dog the more jealous he felt but also the more determined he becomes. The dog was playing rough. His daddy sat down and put the dog on the ground. The dog stood next to Adam and looked. The boy stood there for a while without falling to the ground. No one said anything. The dog sat down next to Adam and looked on. The boy looked at the dog and quickly cast a quick glance at his daddy. He eyed the dog again and his dad. In a flash, he started running toward his daddy. He looked at him and briefly at the dog. He was surprised to see the dog sat there without running to knock him down. The boy looked at his dad and ran. A few feet from the ultimate point the boy stumbled and staggered before falling. He got up and frowned touching his hand. Instantly the dog ran after him and pushed him to get up before standing next to him barking. He looked at his father who this time had stood up. The dog set off but just a few steps ahead before coming back and setting off again next to the boy. The boy got the idea and smiled looking at the dog and then his father. He got up and ran as fast as he can and before touching the finishing line his dad had already lifted him high. The dog barked circling the two. The family celebrated. The boy laughed before his dad put him down then the dog jumped on him and wriggled its tail. A man walked to them and looked at them.

"What a strong boy, resilient and persistent just like his father only if he doesn't end up dead."

Adam frowned and looked at the man. He quickly lifted his boy.

"Who are you?"

"Just a friend. I am just saying it would be a pity for this boy to grow up without his father."

"Don't threaten me. I don't even know you."

"You don't need to know me but him."

The man pointed at a man surrounded by other men further down the park.

"Who is he supposed to be?"

The man laughed and tried to touch his baby.

"Leave my son out of this. Is that who I think it is?"

"Everyone knows that man."

"What does he want?"

"Why not go and ask him yourself?"

Adam carried his son and walked away from the
man. The dog barked at the men before following
Adam. Present-day. In a house in one of the
suburbs, Anita slumped onto the bed nude and Joe
got up and reached for his laptop.

"How long shall we go on like this? I think there are
more people now after us than just Viktor."

"What makes you say that?"

"The man who tried to kill me surely he was not
Viktor's man. He was that sophisticated that he
nearly killed me. He was too fast and advanced. He
knew how to reset himself."

"We must be safe here. This used to be my daddy's
house. He has been gone for years." "You never
mentioned your dad before." Joe jumped on the bed
and looked at Anita with an excited face followed
by a sad face. Anita drove the Lamborghini out of
the building so fast spinning the car around before
hitting the road very hard. She looked in the view
rear mirror and instantly she pressed hard on the
brakes and the car stopped instantly and she revved
the car and looked at her face in the side mirror. She
looked at her eyes which had turned red due to
crying, all the mascara was now smudged. She

remained stationary looking in the rear-view mirror. She cried, and a tear dropped onto the gear stick. She quickly drove away revving the Lamborghini nearly losing control on one of the corners as it nearly collided with a lorry. She arrived at Joe's father's house. She parked the car and entered the house. She slumped onto the bed and cried. She stood up and looked in the dressing table mirror. All the mascara had been washed off by her tears. She instantly had a flashback and instinctively covered her face before slumping back onto the bed. She remembered talking to Joe. Quickly she grabbed the laptop and entered some information. A message appeared on the screen. She took her purse from the bed and retrieved a small card. She wore her reading glasses and looked at the card. A message appeared on the screen again. She punched in codes into the laptop. After a while, a message finally appeared on the screen that caught her attention. Quickly she wiped off the tears and looked impatiently at the screen. Another message appeared 'Emptying all receiving baskets into the vault,' she cursed.

"What vault. He never talked anything about the vault."

Anita stood up and paced left and right in the bedroom. She slumped onto the bed looking upward. She quickly had a flashback and closed her eyes. She cried and then a beep sound went off from the laptop. She quickly got up and sat down and looked at the screen.

"The vault is fully loaded please empty first before any transactions can be processed. Press enter to confirm."

She quickly pressed the enter button. "Please enter the holding account."

"Anita took her purse again and fast emptied everything onto the bed and took out her account. Quickly she entered the account in a hurry missing one digit in the process. She pressed the enter button and waited.

"Incorrect account number."

Was the automated message displayed?

"I knew it. All this was a game. Just a fucking game. You died for nothing. I wish you were here."

She picked up the empty purse and hit the dressing table mirror. She cried profusely before another beep caught her attention. "Second attempt. Please enter the holding account." She crawled down and looked for the card. She picked up the card, and this time entered the digits one by one checking all the digit. She looked again and again before pressing the enter button. A circle soon appeared on the screen. The circle moved clockwise for some minutes. Anita looked and waited hoping for the best. She lay on the bed thinking about Joe and how things had turned. She felt like crying. A beep from the laptop sends her jumping onto the bed landing on her knees.

"The virtual vault is now empty. $100 billion has been transferred to the virtual holding account until processing is complete."

"$100 billion! $100 billion! $100 billion!" Whispered Anita to herself before jumping up and down on the bed. When she thought about Joe, she slumped onto the bed. She held in tears. Quickly she looked for the things the few she really needed and took her cards and the laptop. She quickly changed and took the car keys and left the bedroom before briefly coming back to the bedroom. She opened the knickers drawer and took out a gun, checked it if it was loaded and headed out of the house down the stairs before pushing the door open. Instantly a shot was fired missing her head by inches.

"My men never misses. Cooperate or die. I hope you know how much I dislike being lied to."

Shouted the President as he got out of one of the black SUVs.

"I understand my friend left something for me in your possessions. I need the bank card. If you don't waste my time, I will spare your life."

Lights were shone at her and guns pointed at her. She raised her hands and threw everything down.

"Move away from your belongings stand clear where I can see you. Don't try anything stupid or I will shoot you." Shouted one of the security servicemen. She moved away until the man knelt. Instantly she pulled the gun from her back and pointed at the President.

"Very stupid. My men will exterminate you before you even had the chance to blink. Put your gun down," smiled the President. "I know you very well Mr. President."

The President paused for a while.

"Have we met before?"

"You can say that."

The President sounded angry.

"I dislike being lied to. My memory serves me right. I never met you before."

The security servicemen looked at the President and signaled that they have her. They can take her out before she shoots him. The President raised his hand. "Where have we met before? Don't worry I won't kill you. I promise I just want the truth from you."

"Let's just say I can still feel your hands around my neck."

The President looked shocked and instantly he couldn't breathe with rage and anger.

"I thought she was taken care of. What am I paying you for?" Kai approached the President.

"Stanley was right there was someone outside."

"Why didn't you clean her that day?"

"She mouse-trapped-blind Kai," explained Stanley The President shook with rage. "Shoot her right now."

"No. If you shoot you won't ever get the $100 billion."

"I don't care. After all, this kid here will talk. Shoot her."

"No. No. No please wait I put the gun down. Take the money. What kid are you talking about?"

The President raised his hand. One of his men opened the boot and lifted Joe out before throwing him onto the ground. He groaned and when Anita heard his voice she screamed and ran toward him. She lay on top of him.

"Joe! Joe! Joe! Oh, Joe! I thought you were dead. How did you survive? She touched Joe all over checking for wounds."

The President walked back to one of the SUVs and raised his hand. He walked a few steps and stood. The men aimed their guns and instantly the President yelled.

"Don't shoot let them go."

"Mr. President. They know too much. Unnecessary risk."

"Mr. President you are making a mistake." The President searched for the door handle before entering the SUV.

"I gave my word."

"But."

"$1 billion for every man here. Let's go." Anita cried and laughed at the same time. "Why didn't you run? I made it clear for you to run?"

"What are you talking about? I don't want any money. I gave all the money up. Let's go somewhere far away. We can start all over just you and me. Last night was the best night of my life sleeping next to you." Joe looked at Anita.

"I am too young for you."

"Coward just making an excuse. How about I love you too?"

"I don't even know what love is."

"It doesn't matter. I can't let you die on me again."

"I want to be with you."

"So, let's go to France I have relatives there. Anywhere I don't care as long as I am with you." Anita knelt on her knees on the bed and tickled Joe's hair.

"I thought you died. Still, now I can't understand how you survived those bullets."

Joe looked at her and smiled.

"My guardian angel is dying too." Frantically Anita asked so many questions crying and hugging Joe.

"What are you talking about? If you were to die, you should have died by now. The wounds have already healed."

"Something died too."

Joe touched his heart.

"I am your new love. Your new heart. Your guardian angel. Whatever you want me to be. Okay."

"I died that day."

"What do you mean?"

A tear ran down Joe's cheek. Anita kissed him
passionately all over.

"You ran away and left me."

"What was I supposed to do. Joe! Joe! Tell me!"
Anita cried hugging Joe.

"I am sorry. I am not as strong as you." "You should
have stayed with me." Anita stopped and thought
for a while.

"Joe, we could all have been shot dead." Joe looked
at Anita and smiled.

"Someone saved my life, but he or she is dying
too."

"What do you want me to do?"

"Hug me I will tell you a story."

"A man took to the park his son and his dog to play.
He played with his son. He watched his son
complete his ever first marathon. This was his best
day since the day his son was born. The man
quickly got interrupted. Soon after everything
turned bad for the man. He came back to find his
dog missing.

"I am listening," said Anita.

"This man discovered the great discovery of the century."

Joe kissed Anita and smoothly caressed her body.

"The man discovered that the government is not what it seems. The government is way corrupt than what everyone knows it today. The government is like a business entity just there to make money for the leader the President and a few of his mates.

"We all know that they are crooks."

"This is way above what any human knows."

"Really are you sure it can be worse than it is?"

"Listen to this."

Anita hugged him very tight.

"The government is like a pyramid. You know."

"Excuse me. Pyramid,"

"Yes, a naked scheme pyramid. You know these so-called money schemes."

"I don't believe you."

"I know and the rest of the world."

"It's so sophisticated that no one will ever know what goes on behind those doors." "Genius, huh?"

"Not me just lucky to inherit some wicked genes."

"Let me guess. Dad."

"Honestly I think both."

"OK just like a pyramid eventually everyone at the bottom losses meaning they don't get anything. All those who vote for the President are the eventual losers. They put in effort, sweat, you name it, but they are not guaranteed to anything. Common knowledge with these pyramids." "Fairly fine and common."

"The President has to come up with a way of raising a lot of money. I am talking about $ trillions which if he pressed the correct buttons and chose the right people to cover the top pyramid. The people he can trust and people willing to die for him to cover up for him."

"So, we are talking about best friends, relatives and girlfriends, and boyfriends' husbands and wives. Joe who will do such a thing line up Washington with his buddies and relatives?"

"Exactly a few courage enough to do that. That's why a few people like us are one in a billion."

"Just like a pyramid. It must be the shortest time one should be in the office. This is where it gets interesting. The President chooses how much he wants. In $ billions and for the few brave ones who are willing to kill for their money even $ trillions."

"Joe is this for real?"

"Listen first. The President takes office and on the first day, he must tell the reserve bank how much money will be enough for him to run the government successfully, say $10 trillion. The reserve bank will automatically virtually make that money available. They print the money you know but first the money will be virtual. The President is given access to the money and a bank account."

"Waal on his first day he has all that money to himself. Only if he can take the money with him after serving the government." Joe opened his eyes.

"From the first day in the office, you are already a Trillionaire. Yours to take with a few of your buddies."

"I don't believe you why all these Presidents look miserable after office?" "Bigger brain Anita. Being President is a chance to go into the office and say I am the President of the United States. I am going to print $10 trillion for myself. After I served your ass and did everything you ask me, I will take the money and share with my close buddies whilst all losers get fuck-all. In other words, for me to do all this I will charge you labor in tones of $10 trillion dollars, but no one will know about this. But the trick is that he won't touch or use that money is still in office. He must come up with ideas to generate funds enough to match his initial demand. In this case, he has to look for an investment that will generate $10 trillion dollars' worth of investment."

"Now I see why it's hard to achieve." "There are a lot of things they can do. First, they can form alliances with anyone they want. In fact, anyone if they generate enough wealth to cover their initial figure. Example. They might wage war to get cheaper oil. Soldiers die, civilians die, and the government will payout to the estates of the victims and soldiers but in the long run, they make great achievements or improve certain sectors of the industry say aviation as they now get cheaper jet fuel. That increases the wealth of the economy. Those who understand this will do whatever it takes to source resources, create business links that add value to the economy whatever, to try to build up the wealth using the country current resources."

"So, but still makes no sense the money is just virtual money after all. It can easily disappear."

"Not so right. Two weeks into office the physical money is printed and taken to a building of the President's choice. Where only him and the treasury know about. It's then up to him to communicate with his supporters and members of the government where the money is and how they can get the money. They have five years to acquire the building and take the money."

"If they don't?"

"The place will be blown up or, for example, one day you will come back to take the money away and found out that the school had been replaced by a huge building." "That would be something."

"So, Joe are you saying that from the first day in office until the day he leaves the money is his fair and fine?"

"His all the way."

"What happens let's say he gets the money at the end?" Joe smiled.

"It's his, he has to give the Secretary of the Treasure the virtual money card, so his money can be made official and injected into the system. Making everything legal." "If that's easy why they all fail?" "Misunderstanding, greedy but if my father was here, he would say just mankind stupidity. The people gave you all the resources in the country including themselves. If you can't make yourself a wealth when you have all the resources to your name, then how on earth are you able to run the country?"

"Damn man you are good. I never thought of it that way."

"My father used to say I will lend you $10 make yourself a dollar or more but I want my $10 back."

"So why do they all fail?"

"First, they choose lesser amounts at the beginning and throughout the five years just go with the floor. Two, they throw away I mean forget people who have stuck out their necks for them once they are at White house. They abandon all those close to them and instead choose strangers to be the best people. Three they stay too long in power. No one ever resigns within their first term. Most push for a second term in office. Just a waste. In the second term, books fail to balance. $ trillions start going missing, in the end, the money is forcibly blown up. Total failure."

Anita suddenly jumped up and down and knelt near Joe.

"Answer this Joe."

"Go ahead."

"The $100 billion I transferred is it the virtual money of the hidden cash? Joe! Is it Answer me?"

Anita's face shone as she looked excited. "That's different but I believe the last $trillions haven't been found nor the virtual card been handed in."

"But I thought the card is handed at the end of service whether you take the money or not?"

"True."

"So?"

Joe took a long breath.

"The man was killed a day before his term in office ended before he had the chance to hand back the card. Luckily, he had given the card to his best friend a day before he died that is two days before the end of his term in office. Sadly, his friend was killed too after he had given the card to his son after the park incident."

"What are you saying? Joe come on talk to me."

"Joe what did I tell you about lying to your mother and your half-sister for that matter."

Joe and Anita looked at the man standing at the door wearing scruffy clothes and having a long beard. Instantly Joe had a flashback the day he was at the park with his dad. He remembered getting jealous as the dog got all the attention. He remembered falling and being tripped by the dog every time he tried to reach his dad. He also remembered the time the dog and his dad cheered on him as he lay on the ground. Anita got up and knelt next to the man. The two started cheering up Joe applauding.

"Joe! Joe! Joe! Joe! Joe," Joe felt a tear running down his cheeks. Followed by another tear and then another.

"Daddy! Daddy!" The three hugged together and danced around.

"Daddy. They told me you died. If I knew you were alive, surely, I could have looked for you. So, all along it was you. The car and everything? Where is mum?" Joe's father looked at Joe.

"Surprise."

A small dog exactly like the one Joe had before as a kid ran into the room and licked Joe everywhere. A woman stood at the door.

"Mum! Mum!"

The five hugged each other. The dog barked and licked Joe.

"Daddy what about the money I need at least 25%?"

"What it's not even my money why you ask me? Why can't you ask Anita your sister the rightful owner of the money?"

"Half-sister." Corrected Joe's mother. "Half-brother. Ewe. Forget about the money. You are not getting any.,"

Yelled Anita.

"Mum she cried for me. She said that she doesn't care about the money. She just wanted to take me to France." Shouted Joe. "He tricked me I thought he was dying and technically I can't marry my brother, can I?"

"Half-brother."

Corrected Joe's mother.

"Speaking of blind dates. You are a couple now."

"But you said she is my half-sister?"

"Do you believe everything I tell you?" "Excuse me. I am not happy to be your wife either."

"Go on a honeymoon somewhere nice. France."

"France. OK, dad as long as she is the one paying."

To be continued...

THE END

ABOUT CAROLINADEIVID

I am a new author with a new-age writing style that aims to keep you the reader hooked until the end of the book and even after leaving you gagging for more. Buy my next book. Thank You.

Carolinadeivid

Carolinadeivid